BUFFY
X-POSED

TED EDWARDS

BUFFY X-POSED

The Unauthorized Biography
of Sarah Michelle Gellar
and Her On-Screen Character

PRIMA PUBLISHING

Library of Congress Cataloging-in-Publication Data

Edwards, Ted.
    Buffy x-posed : the unauthorized biography of Sarah Michelle Gellar and her on-screen character / Ted Edwards.
      p.   cm.
    Includes index.
    ISBN 0-7615-1368X
    1. Gellar, Sarah Michelle 1977–.   2. Actors—United States—Biography.
I. Title.
PN2287.G46C74   1998
792'.028'092— dc21
[b]   98-19144
                                                     CIP

   99 00 01 02 03 DD 10 9 8 7 6 5 4 3
Printed in the United States of America

HOW TO ORDER
Single copies may be ordered from Prima Publishing, P.O. Box 1260BK, Rocklin, CA 95677; telephone (916) 632-4400. Quantity discounts are also available. On your letterhead, include information concerning the intended use of the books and the number of books you wish to purchase.

Visit us online at http://www.primapublishing.com

CONTENTS

contents

BUFFY X-POSED:
AN INTRODUCTION

Buffy the Vampire Slayer.

Just the name itself is so goofy-sounding that it runs the risk of being a turn-off as a television show. This is especially true when one realizes that it's based on a pretty awful feature film of the same name, which was an unsuccessful mix of humor and horror.

Of course, one should not get too hung up on titles because, in reality, *Buffy the Vampire Slayer* is one hell of a TV show, proving itself to be everything that the feature film was intended to be but couldn't quite achieve. Considering that the show is guided by writer Joss Whedon, who also scripted the film and has gone on record regarding how much he despises it, it's no surprise. *Buffy,* the TV show, testifies to a reality that Hollywood is loathe to admit: that, in many instances, the writer truly does know best. Whedon deserves a lot of credit for coming up with a unique concept and having the creative ability to pull it off on a weekly basis. He is also blessed with a hell of a writing staff and a first-rate cast of young actors, most notably former soap opera star Sarah Michelle Gellar, Nicholas Brendon, Alyson Hannigan, Charisma Carpenter, David Boreanaz, and Anthony Stewart Head. This particular combination of writers and actors has managed to create magic.

Timing probably has a lot to do with it, too. Whedon launched the series on the WB at roughly the same time that the horror genre came back in full force, thanks to such efforts as *Scream, I Know What You Did Last Summer,* and *Scream 2,* all of which contain the same balance of humor and horror that distinguishes the TV series. Simultaneously, vampires themselves seem to be on the verge of a major comeback, with the Wesley Snipes starrer *Blade* and John Carpenter's *Vampires.*

BUFFY X-POSED: AN INTRODUCTION

Buffy X-Posed is the first guide to this series, featuring biographies of Sarah Michelle Gellar, her supporting cast, and Joss Whedon, as well as a complete guide to the show's first two seasons, highlighted by credits, airdates, summaries, and critical examinations. In addition, look for a couple of appendices that examine previous entries in the vampire genre.

Hope you enjoy the material we've staked out for you.

Albert L. Ortega

Albert L. Ortega

vision & Radio

Albert L. Ortega

Albert L. Ortega

Albert L. Ortega

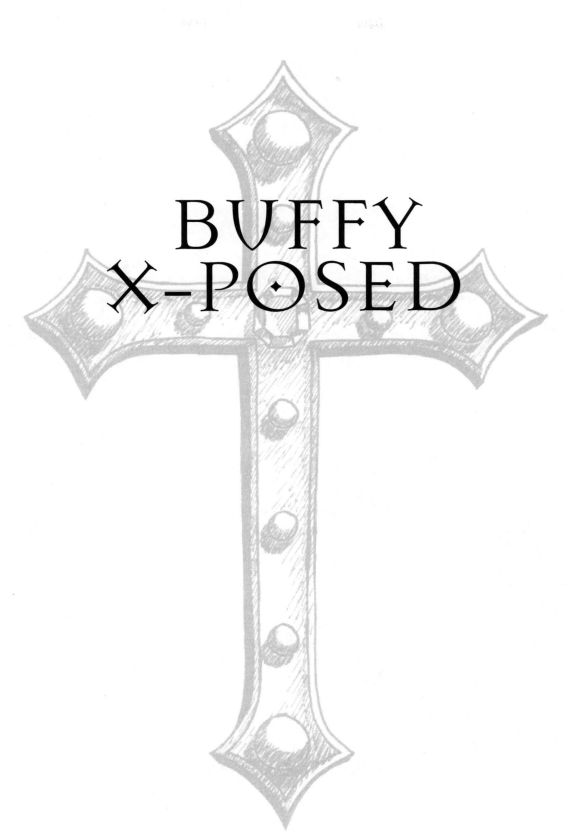

BUFFY
X-POSED

CHAPTER ONE

SARAH MICHELLE GELLAR

*From Soap Star
to Vampire Slayer*

When four-year-old Sarah Michelle Gellar began acting in television commercials, the notion of slaying vampires was the furthest thing from her mind. But now, a decade and a half later, that's exactly how she spends her evenings. Truthfully, though, there are a hell of a lot of worse ways to make ends meet.

In its third season, *Buffy the Vampire Slayer* has become the biggest hit of the fledgling WB network, propelling past anything offered by UPN and seriously challenging the series fare airing opposite it on the other networks. Perhaps most impressive about this achievement is that the show was based on a failed motion picture and was initially perceived by critics and audiences as an *X-Files* wannabe. Almost from the start, though, *Buffy* proved itself to be something quite different—as did Gellar.

Gellar's career quite literally began at a restaurant, where the four-year-old was having lunch with a playmate. Reflected Gellar in an amalgamation of several interviews, "It was one of those fluke incidents," she said. "I was sitting in a restaurant and had just learned my name and my address. This woman walked up to me and asked if I'd like to be on television. I was like, 'Yeah, OK. My name is Sarah Michelle Gellar, I live at . . . ,' and I gave her my address. I didn't know what I was doing. It probably wasn't the smartest thing. . . . I don't do it anymore. I did stop. The woman called my mother, and my mother thought it was just a joke, a prank. Then she sent me on a

"THERE ARE A LOT OF ACTORS WHO HAVE BEEN WORKING SINCE A YOUNG AGE AND THEY'RE JUST FINE. MY STEPFATHER ALWAYS SAYS THAT WHEN HE SEES HOW MANY THINGS I HANDLE IN A DAY, HE'D BE WILLING TO HIRE A YOUNG PERSON LIKE ME BECAUSE HE SEES WHAT AN INCREDIBLE THING IT IS TO SEE KIDS SO FOCUSED AND HOW MUCH THEY HAVE TO OFFER."
—SARAH MICHELLE GELLAR

movie audition a week later and I got it. The whole time my mom's thinking, 'That's nice, honey, go play,' and I'm thinking, 'No, I'm going to be on TV, Mom, really.' And she's looking at me like I'm insane."

That movie was a TV film called *An Invasion of Privacy*, which starred Valerie Harper, Richard Masur, Jerry Orbach, Carol Kane, and Jeff Daniels—not too shabby a beginning for a kid setting out on the road to stardom. "It had an amazing cast," Gellar enthused on *The Tonight Show*. "Valerie Harper played my mom and it was an amazing experience." Of her audition for the film, she added, "I was supposed to read with Valerie Harper, but she had already gone home, so I said, 'No problem.' First I did my lines and then, in Valerie's voice, I did hers. I was hired on the spot."

Burger King came calling soon afterward, casting Gellar as a child who performs the unprecedented act of saying that her product was better than the competition's—and McDonald's was actually mentioned by name! Reflecting on those commercials, Gellar commented, "I was the little Burger King girl that couldn't say the word 'burger.' It sort of came out 'bugah.' Usually they like you to be able to pronounce the product you're representing. But they did send me for speech lessons and eventually I could speak and say the word 'burger.' I was about five to seven when I did them, and I did about thirty commercials. What I said [in the commercial] was, 'Do I look 20 percent smaller to you? I must to McDonald's because their hamburgers are 20 percent smaller,' which everyone knows is true. So I said that and McDonald's didn't know what to do because no one had ever done it before. So McDonald's

Albert L. Ortega

THE SLAYER BEGAN HER CAREER AS A
FOUR-YEAR-OLD PITCH KID FOR BURGER KING.

turned around and sued Burger King and sued J. Walter Thompson, the advertising company, and sued me—at five. There were these big lawyers and little me, at five. I didn't even know how to say the word 'lawyer.' I was calling it 'layuh.' It was very weird to be that young and be called in as a witness. A few months later I was telling my friends, 'I can't play, I've got to give a deposition.' And, of course, when you're five years old, where do all your friends have birthday parties? I was going to birthday parties at five years old wearing a big straw hat and sunglasses, because I couldn't really go to McDonald's—truth in advertising."

The case was ultimately settled out of court, just as Gellar settled on her decision to become a real actress. Even as a child, she worked hard to develop her craft and continued to go out on auditions, at first scoring a variety of television commercials. This put an enormous amount of pressure on the elementary school student. "What happened," she explained, "is that I was going to school, acting, skating, and doing Tae Kwon Do all at one time. No human being can do that, and my mom's rule was, if my grades got below an A-, I had to stop working. So she sat down one day and said, 'You can pick

two things, you can't do them all. And,' she said, 'school has to be one of them.' So I chose acting. And now it's great, 'cause I get to use the Tae Kwon Do in the show and I'm learning kick boxing and boxing and street fighting. Plus, I get to run around like a lunatic. The truth is, I was not meant to be in Little League or the local ballet school. I'm tired of people who say, 'Acting corrupts these young people.' You know what? There are a lot of actors who have been working since a young age and they're just fine. My stepfather always says that when he sees how many things I handle in a day, he'd be willing to hire a young person like me because now he sees what an incredible thing it is to see kids so focused and how much they have to offer."

Beginning in 1980, Gellar made the transition from commercials to television guest spots. It began with an appearance as a flower girl on the CBS daytime soap opera *Guiding Light*. She followed with an episode of the syndicated *William Tell* series, the Tony Randall NBC sitcom *Love Sidney* (controversial, in that Randall was playing the first gay character to appear on a regular TV series), and Robert Urich's ABC private eye series *Spenser: For Hire.* In 1989 Gellar served as a co-host of the syndicated teen show *Girl Talk,* before costarring in the teen soap opera *Swan's Crossing.* She managed to secure a fairly big break for herself as the young Jackie Bouvier in the 1991 TV movie *A Woman Named Jackie.* As Gellar told the *Washington Post,* "High school life was good, but junior high was my Buffy experience—I hated it. I was the girl nobody liked, who was weird and quirky. That's another reason I can relate to Buffy. I also preferred acting. In one grade I had more absences in the first month than you're supposed to have in an entire year. I was telling them I had back problems

Albert L. Ortega

FROM PITCHING BURGERS TO CONQUERING THE ENTERTAINMENT WORLD.

and had to go to doctors all the time—then *A Woman Named Jackie* aired."

In between, she managed to play minor roles in the features *Over the*

"HIGH SCHOOL LIFE WAS GOOD, BUT JUNIOR HIGH WAS MY BUFFY EXPERIENCE—I HATED IT. I WAS THE GIRL NOBODY LIKED, WHO WAS WEIRD AND QUIRKY. THAT'S ANOTHER REASON I CAN RELATE TO BUFFY."

—SARAH MICHELLE GELLAR

"*All My Children* was my first job when I started taking it seriously," she told Jay Leno, "when it became a career, and it was such an amazing job! I think I was a good character; I go with misunderstood. I had a busy first week. I locked my little sister in the crypt, burned my parents' divorce papers, tried to seduce my stepfather, and when he turned me down I slept with the stable boy, then cried rape and went to jail. It was a good first week."

In various interviews, Gellar reflected on her two years' working on the soap opera. "I thank Judy Wilson [the show's casting director] so much for giving me the chance to actually be a teenager playing a teenager on the show," she said. "In this business, if you're a young person who doesn't look like you're in your forties, it's really hard to get a role with any meat to it. To get a role like Kendall, I feel so

Brooklyn Bridge (1984), Chevy Chase's *Funny Farm* (1988), and *High Stakes* (1989). As if this wasn't enough, Gellar also squeezed in a role in Neil Simon's Broadway play *Jake's Women* and costarred with Matthew Broderick in a Circle in the Square production of *The Widow Claire.*

Undoubtedly, her biggest break was being cast as Kendall Hart, Erica Kane's (Susan Lucci) daughter, on the daytime soap *All My Children.* Gellar was all of fifteen at the time.

lucky because it's so rare. They just don't write for kids anymore. You always have older people playing younger people. I'm sorry, but *90210?* Hello! I go to school and our seniors sure don't look like that! There are some very talented teenagers who can do just as good, if not better, than any adults, but they're not given a fair chance. But Kendall Hart is definitely the most terrible daughter on daytime. I don't always agree with her methods, but as an actress I have to justify her actions—and I do. I didn't know when I auditioned for Kendall that she would turn out to be who she is. I had heard rumors, but they were squelched very quickly. I was scared enough just to be working with Susan, and then when they told me I would be playing [Susan Lucci's] daughter, I was like, 'I'm her WHAT? Daughter? Me?'"

Gellar's work ethic and maturity beyond her seventeen years simultaneously surprised and confounded some of her co-stars on the soap. *All My Children*'s Eva La Rue offered to *Soap Opera Digest,* "Sarah's like a forty-year-old woman trapped in a seventeen-year-old body. She's wise way beyond her years. [But she loved talking on the phone.] There was one morning when she came to work exhausted because she'd been up to 3:00 in the morning talking to friends. When I asked her why she didn't just turn the ringer off and go to bed, she said, 'I'm a teenager. I'm supposed to talk on the phone for hours.' It was like being slapped in the face by reality. She's so mature that it's easy to forget she's only seventeen years old."

One of the co-stars who did *not* share warm feelings for Gellar was her on-screen mother, Susan Lucci. Although details were never fully disclosed to the press, Lucci reportedly felt that she was being upstaged by the younger actress and, by some accounts, did not make things easy for her. The situation wasn't helped when Geller, after telling the producers she was planning to leave the soap two years in, was nominated for a daytime Emmy, which she ultimately won. Lucci, as is well-known, has been nominated seventeen times but has *never* won.

"It was not the easiest situation on the show," she told *Rolling Stone.* "I'm

Ron Davis/Shooting Star

GELLAR WON AN EMMY FOR HER STINT ON
<u>ALL MY CHILDREN</u>. HER TV MOM, SUSAN
LUCCI, HAS NOT MANAGED TO DO THE SAME.

Emmy was a wonderful . . . well, I don't want to say vindication." Gellar added in *People,* "[Susan Lucci] and I didn't do lunch on weekends. We weren't girlfriends shopping together. It wasn't the easiest working relationship. But the stories were blown out of proportion."

She also had to deal with some bad press when, almost immediately after winning the Emmy, she announced that she was leaving *All My Children* to pursue other acting opportunities. "It made me look incredibly bad," she related to *People.* "I was told by ABC that I couldn't announce my leaving until they made an official announcement. The timing was terrible. The only way to look at it—and this is what I said to Susan—is that I won for work we did together."

being polite by not saying what I'd like to say. I've always taken the high road. It's hard at sixteen to understand some adult things at that point. Winning the

Of her soap opera tenure, she noted, "The soap in general for me was an up and a down. Those were hard years. I was fifteen to seventeen, I graduated high school two years early during that time. I was growing up. It was a very awkward time. And, for me, the Emmy was a validation of the work that I'd done and the time that I spent there. But at the same time, I was ready to move on. For many reasons, one of them being just the fact that two years in the life of a fifteen-year-old or an eighteen-year-old is a very long time. And, when I got to LA, I really had to start from scratch. And so, the Emmy, to me, was the culmination of my soap years."

Gellar's next big break was auditioning for, and getting, the role of Buffy Summers in the WB series *Buffy*

"THERE WAS NO SECOND PLACE. WE READ TONS OF PEOPLE AND SEVERAL WERE STAGGERINGLY UNTALENTED. BUFFY IS A TOUGH PART. IT IS A CHARACTER ACTRESS IN THE PART OF A LEADING LADY. . . . FINDING BUFFY WAS THE BIGGEST CHALLENGE, AND I THINK IF WE HADN'T FOUND SARAH, THE SERIES MIGHT NOT HAVE HAPPENED OR LASTED."
—SERIES CREATOR JOSS WHEDON

the Vampire Slayer, a fascinating hybrid of the horror/action/comedy genres. "My manager spoke to Warner Bros. network and they mentioned they had this Buffy show," she told *Femme Fatales.* "He thought it would be a great opportunity to use my Tae Kwan Do and do

Chip Eli/Shooting Star

FROM THE MOMENT SHE STAKED OUT THE ROLE OF BUFFY, GELLAR MADE IT HER OWN.

script and heard about Joss Whedon and how wonderful he was. I went to the audition the week he was Oscar nominated for his *Toy Story* screenplay. I thought, 'I'm going to have this role.' He tells me I nailed it, but I still went through eleven auditions."

Added Whedon, "There was no second place. We read tons of people and several were staggeringly untalented. Buffy is a tough part. It is a character actress in the part of a leading lady. This girl has to look the part of the blonde bimbo who dies in reel two, and yet she's not that. Buffy is a very loopy, very funny, very strange person—kind of eccentric. Sarah has all those qualities and you don't find them in a beautiful, young girl very often. She gave us a reading that was letter

comedy and drama. I probably had eleven auditions and four tests. It was the most awful experience of my life, but I was so driven. I had read the perfect and then said, 'By the way, it doesn't say this on my resume, but I did take Tae Kwon Do for four years and I'm a brown belt. Is that good?' 'No, perfect.' Finding Buffy was the biggest challenge, and I think if we hadn't found Sarah, the series might not have happened or lasted. What Sarah brings to the part is her intelligence. At the same time, she's got the hormonal idiosyncratic goofiness that makes Buffy not just the Terminator. She approaches the vampires with total irreverence, which drives them crazy. I call her Jimmy Stewart because she suffers so well."

At the same time, Gellar has given Whedon anxiety attacks on more than one occasion, particularly in terms of her zealousness in handling many of her own stunts. "My attitude," Whedon told *Movie Aliens,* "is that the show isn't so good that it's worth anybody getting hurt for it. Sarah is always covered with bruises and I'm always saying, 'Sarah, don't do this stuff. We'll get the close-up of you saying the funny thing after.' 'No, no, I can do it,' she says, and then she gets this giant black-and-blue-mark on her arm. 'Sarah, stop. Please!'"

"When I was growing up, and not to knock these shows," Gellar told *The Detroit Free Press,* "I watched Mallory worry about her dates and her boyfriends on *Family Ties.* I watched Blair on *Facts of Life.* There were no strong characters. I'm sorry, Tootie was not a role model, y'know? But with *Buffy,* we're showing real situations. Buffy is not the prettiest girl in her school, she's not the most popular, she's not the smartest. She makes mistakes, she makes good decisions and bad decisions. She's dealing with real situations that we put on a fantasy level." In *Venice* magazine she added, "As an actor, you can always bring parts of yourself to characters, but hopefully it's only a small portion of it, and the rest is a new character that you developed. My junior high school was like Buffy's. I was kind of a nerd. I didn't have many friends and I was an outcast. But I think Buffy is an amazing role model because the one thing that I was able to do at my high school was be an individual. The problem with most high schools is they don't stress individuality. Buffy shows girls it's okay to be different."

Gellar's first efforts as Buffy were showcased in a half-hour "presentation" of the series that preceded the show's pilot and was written and directed by executive producer Joss Whedon. The primary purpose of this presentation was to interest the executives of the WB in the idea of *Buffy* as a series. "That was Joss's first directing experience and he didn't have a very good support team behind him," said Gellar. "We didn't know what we were doing with the show. It was like all these ideas in your head and they're not working out right on paper. We had a whole summer to fix it by the time we did the real pilot, and I think we did a pretty good job. What made everything work is we needed to find Alyson Hannigan. She was the best and what allowed Nicholas Brendon and myself to become a threesome. Once she came aboard, everything clicked."

Interestingly, once *Buffy* was given the green light for series production, the show was designed for a midseason debut. This meant that Whedon and his cast and crew would be producing the first twelve episodes without any feedback whatsoever from either the critics or the audience.

"We finished the entire first season before we went on the air, so we were able to do it in a bubble without having anybody on the outside interfering," she explained. "When I was in North Carolina [shooting *I Know What You Did Last Summer*], we didn't get to see it because it was on a cable channel we couldn't get in the town we were in. I was able to avoid the craziness, although Alyson called me every week, going, 'You don't understand, every time you go past a grocery store there's a *Buffy* billboard.'"

Over the course of several interviews, Gellar detailed her feelings about the series. "The network wasn't exactly sure what we were doing in the beginning. After the praying-mantis episode, they said, 'We're just not sure if we're sending the right message.' We're like, 'What message? You have sex with her and she bites your head off.' These are situations that children can relate to; the themes throughout the show are common: loving a friend, being at an age when you're having problems with Mom, and wanting to be an adult and wanting to be a child at the same time. The scariest horror exists in reality. It's feeling so invisible, date rape, these are situations teenagers understand and can relate to because it's happening to them," she said. "This is very different from the movie. What we did was take the concept of the movie of this sixteen-year-old girl who is popular and has a perfect life, but there is something missing and she feels the kind of sixteen-year-old aching that everyone felt in their adolescence: Am I an adult? Am I a child? And, suddenly, she has to save the world. Now she's an outcast. She

Jay Blakesbery/Retna Limited USA

GELLAR VAMPING AS THE SUN RISES.

doesn't fit in. She doesn't know if she wants to be a cheerleader or fight vampires, and that is what makes her interesting and believable. Buffy is a person

"[Joss] has been totally behind it. . . . Obviously he understands people's desire to do movies and that's how he started. Though he would like me to do a movie for him now, since I've done two Kevin Williamson films."
—Sarah Michelle Gellar

FROM SLAYER TO VICTIM

The success of *Buffy the Vampire Slayer* is a phenomenon that executives from every other network—with the possible exception of Fox—should be forced to analyze. The series debuted with far from stellar ratings. Indeed, in its first season it was the WB's lowest rated show. Despite this, the network stuck with the show and refused to try and force it into being something that the audience *might* like, choosing, instead, to let the series progress naturally, in hopes that the audience would eventually catch on. It was a philosophy NBC had employed (seemingly) centuries ago with such shows as *Cheers*, *Family Ties*, and *Hill Street Blues;* and one that Fox had scored big on with *The X-Files* (which many people seem to forget was a disaster when it first premiered).

who is lost, who doesn't know where she belongs—and you can feel for her. Junior high was my time to feel that I didn't know where I fit. I tried to be a jock. I tried to be cool. And I couldn't find my place. I think that is what Willow, Xander, and Buffy are all going through. That's what makes them such wonderful friends—they are helping each other get through this time."

The strategy paid off, and in its second season *Buffy* climbed the ratings, creating an atmosphere that was only further enhanced by the success of such big-screen efforts as *Scream, I Know What You Did Last Summer,* and *Scream 2* (all three of which have involved screenwriter Kevin Williamson). These, in turn, led to a new incarnation of *Halloween,* a remake of Alfred Hitchcock's masterpiece *Psycho,* and rumors that Joss Whedon is developing a big-screen *Buffy* motion picture to star the series cast (à la summer 1998's movie version of *The X-Files*).

Gellar, who co-starred in *I Know What You Did Last Summer* and *Scream 2,* offered, "One of the things about Joss Whedon and Kevin Williamson both is that they really talk to the generation, and not down to them. And it's been an overlooked generation. In my opinion, I think that in the eighties, horror films became almost comical in a sense. It was almost funny. It was the 'babe' running in the woods; it was decapitation and gore and guts and blood. Truthfully, after a while it's not scary; it's funny. I think the thing about Kevin is

that he scares you and then he makes you laugh, and then he has a really touching scene that you can relate to, and then 'boom,' he scares you. The big thing in *Scream*—it was Neve Campbell's joke—was that in horror films there's always a big-breasted girl that's always running upstairs when she should run outside, and that's what Kevin tries to do. I mean, even though my character of Helen [from *I Know What You Did*] is technically the 'babe' in the woods character. She still does intelligent things; she tries to make decisions. Someone was asking me yesterday, 'How is it that you can run so fast and the killer always catches you?' You know, the killer in horror movies always walks really slowly, and this is exactly what it is: it's panic. Think about it: a man with a hook is going to kill her, she's not thinking about what the smarter thing to do would be. She's panicked. I think she made fairly decent decisions: locking the door, calling the police. She really tried, but the killer is always going to have one up on you because he's calm, he's planning, he's thinking. You expect that in horror

20th Century Fox TV/Shooting Star

BUFFY SUMMERS IS THE ROLE
GELLAR WAS BORN TO PLAY.

explained his approach to horror and how it launched *Scream* and a subsequent sub-genre in the first place. "I sort of have this wicked sense of humor that sort of weaves through everything I do," he explained in an online interview. "But when we first started doing it, no one knew if it was a comedy or a scary movie, and [Dimension Films'] Bob Weinstein knew. He said, 'This is a scary movie.' And I said, 'Yes, it is.' They kept going after all these directors who saw it as a comedy. Finally, we sat down and talked to Wes Craven, and he got it. He clearly knew it was a scary movie. There's humor in it, but no, make no mistake, it's scary."

I Know What You Did Last Summer stars Gellar, Jennifer Love Hewitt, Ryan

movies, but Kevin's been able to make it a little more real."

Williamson, the creative voice behind the WB's *Dawson's Creek,* recently

Phillippe, and Freddie Prinze, Jr., and portrays a frightening accident and its aftermath: a group of high school friends are driving along when they hit, and presumably kill, a man and, acting out of fear, hide the body. The next year, the "dead man" returns, seeking vengeance against those who struck him down and did nothing about it.

In its second season *Buffy* climbed the ratings, creating an atmosphere that was only further enhanced by the success of such big-screen efforts as *Scream*, *I Know What You Did Last Summer*, and *Scream 2*.

Gellar, who portrays beauty queen Helen, added, "I loved the script. When you're a young actress, it's very rare to find characters our age that are this fully developed. These are four really strong, intelligent characters who go through transitions that are really human. And for me, the character of Helen was a real departure, and it was something I really wanted to do."

The film was perceived by Geller to be a bit of a departure for her, and it took some getting used to for her to switch from her previous role as a vampire slayer

"The rest of the cast had already been hired before I came aboard, and so after my first rehearsal with them I was just so in awe," she said. "I literally called my manager later that day and said, 'I'm going to pack my bags because I'm going to get fired.' I do this after every job I get, though. It's funny, because after the read-through of the second season premiere of *Buffy,* I still thought I was getting fired. [Anyway], when I first got down there [in North Carolina], I was still in Buffy mode. The director, Jim Gillespie, would give me notes like, 'Sarah, you're looking too athletic. This is not the triathlon here. You can't hit the guy. Buffy can, Helen can't!' What I did after that is, I would untie my shoes and when I would run, I would put pebbles in my shoes. I got a little more used to it. I'm used to being the aggressor in a fight scene and I hated to be 'flailing,' but when I got into it, it became fun."

Based on Lois Duncan's novel of the same name, *I Know What You Did Last Summer* was fairly different from its source material. "In the book," Gellar explained, "they hit and kill an eight-year-old little boy, which, of course, would make a horror movie, but there is nothing redeemable about four teenagers that hit and kill an eight-year-old boy on a bicycle. The ending was completely different. I would never play a character like the way Helen was in the book. Kevin, though, has this way of writing three-dimensional characters for young people and didn't make her this 'babe in the woods'—like

character. Luckily, we had a week's worth of rehearsals, and Kevin was there every day and Jim was there every day, and we really had a chance to talk about things that we felt would help our characters, and things that didn't work for us. Especially for me, because I'm not your stereotypical blonde. I'm not even a blonde in real life, so to play the quintessential dumb blonde character was a big stretch for me, and I wanted to make sure that she wasn't a joke; that she was funny but that she wasn't a character that you would laugh at.

"It is very rare," she added, "when you play the age I play to see something written that's so strongly developed. In the movie, she makes a transition. She's this girl who grew up solely on her looks and all that was expected of her was to be beautiful, have a perfect boyfriend, be a model, and that's what people gave her. What she realizes, though, is that her looks aren't going to get her through the situation and she needs to be capable of more. Helen in the book never makes that transition."

Gellar's inevitable death scene—no doubt a shock to *Buffy* fans—was made more realistic than it was originally written. The actress gives director Jim Gillespie credit for this; he invested more meaning in the sequence than might have otherwise been there.

"We had lots of talks about that scene," said Gellar. "If some guy is coming at you and this is your last chance, you're going to give it everything you have. I think the thing about stalker movies in general is that when characters run away, it's usually a jiggle scene. 'I'm wearing my tight tank top and I'm not going to stop this bad man.' A lot of what Jim's direction was for us was he didn't want to make a movie about how we all looked. He wanted to make a much more serious movie where you believed the characters and the situations they were in, so when they're in danger you care about them."

Terry Lilly/Shooting Star

SARAH MICHELLE GELLAR
HITS HER MARK.

As if this wasn't enough horror for anyone, Gellar segued from *I Know What You Did* over to *Scream 2*. "The way that it happened," she explained to the on-line *HorrorNet,* "was that we finished *Buffy* and it was about two weeks before it aired. They put me on a press junket for the show, and I heard about *I Know What You Did* and I just went in and auditioned for it. I found out that I got the part the day before *Buffy* aired on March 10th. I went to North Carolina and started filming, and the day that I finished filming *I Know What You Did,* I flew to Atlanta and started *Scream 2,* and then flew back and started *Buffy* again and was doing both."

Elsewhere, she continued, "It's random that I've worked on three things in the horror genre this way. The reason I've worked three jobs is that they have been the most interesting, diverse roles I could find. With this genre that Kevin Williamson and Joss Whedon have created, for everybody it provides action, horror, drama, and comedy. What else can I do? A musical? So, when you're my age, it's the best opportunity. I take jobs for the opportunity and this is what offered me the best work. If I get stuck doing work like this, God help me I should be so lucky."

Scream 2 continues the irreverent tone set by its predecessor, as the events of that film are turned into a feature film called *Stab,* while the "real-life" serial killer starts claiming victims again. In the film, Gellar portrays one of Sidney's (Neve Campbell) sorority sisters. What probably surprised the actress more than anything was the secrecy surrounding the project.

"We got our scripts on James Bond paper," she laughed. "They all had this huge big red stripe on them so you couldn't see the words and you can't xerox them. Then each page is numbered with your own special number. Mine was 3130. Also, every rewrite page you got you had to take your old pages and put them through a paper shredder. And no one had the ending. At the read-through, I thought I didn't have the pages because I wasn't in it, but they didn't give it to anybody—not even Neve or Courtney [Cox]. No one knew. We got it a couple of days before everybody started filming."

One of the most exciting aspects of the project for Gellar, apart from Williamson's script, was the chance to work with genre veteran Wes Craven. "Wes was amazing to work with," she said. "When you talk about someone who really created a genre—he knows every nuance and how to turn your head and hear noises. He makes the smallest thing into these wonderful moments. It was real incredible to have the opportunity to work with him. Unlike so many people who start in one genre that don't progress, he's progressed. He's taken it to this new level and it was incredible to work with a master like that. Let me tell you something else. The way Wes keeps his sets, you're completely in this situation. There's the guy with the

Albert L. Ortega

KRISTY SWANSON PORTRAYED BUFFY IN THE 1992 FEATURE FILM.

ghost mask coming at you, and it's horrific. It's really scary. You're on these ledges, you're running up these stairs, and it's pretty terrifying. And it's

Albert L. Ortega

LUKE PERRY LEFT <u>BEVERLY HILLS 90210</u>
TO HELP SLAY VAMPIRES.

turn around, Wes hides people in different places just to freak you out. And it works. You really feel everybody's terror in this movie."

Like Jim Gillespie before him, Craven had to deal with Gellar's over-zealousness in the fight scenes. "I'd throw punches," she said, "and they'd tell me to try flailing a little bit more. And, of course, I'm thinking, 'But that wouldn't be right.' And then I'd remember, 'Oh, yeah, different story.' Besides, Wes told me not to. Wes said, 'Don't kill the bad man, because then he can't come back for a sequel.'"

Gellar feels enormous gratitude toward Joss Whedon, who worked things out so that she could shoot *Scream 2* during production of *Buffy*'s second season, in much the way that Michael J. Fox shot

pretty easy to get into the mode. Nobody knows the genre better than Wes. Whereas most movies have some guy off camera going 'bang' to make you

VAMPIRE SLAYER: MOVIE STYLE

The feature film version of *Buffy the Vampire Slayer* is an annoying movie, taking what could have been a unique premise and completely diluting it by going the camp route at almost every turn (vampire gets hit with a stake and mutters, "I'm pissed;" dead teens are confronted by the school principal, who hands them detention slips; and so forth).

In the film, Buffy is essentially a Valley Girl by day and a vampire slayer by night. Initially, Buffy is reluctant to accept her destiny, until she is made to realize that she has actually been slaying vampires for centuries in previous lives. She is joined in her quest to rid her town of vampires (the leader of which is portrayed by Rutger Hauer, with his undead servant portrayed by Paul "Pee Wee Herman" Reubans) by the town bad boy (Luke Perry) and guided in her actions by her "Watcher" (Donald Sutherland).

Although Sarah Michelle Gellar has obviously made the role of Buffy her own, the character was first portrayed by Kristy Swanson. Despite the too-light touch offered by director Fran Rubel Kuzui, Swanson was able to successfully convey the character's growth from being an airhead Valley Girl to a vampire slayer (unlike the TV spin-off, the film's Buffy only takes on vampires and no other supernatural creatures).

Born in 1969 in Mission Viejo, California, Swanson began appearing in a variety of television commercials at the age of nine. She ultimately parlayed that into a film career, appearing in such efforts as *Ferris Bueller's Day Off, Mannequin 2: On the Move, The Chase, Deadly Friend, Hot Shots, Diving In, Eight Heads in a Duffel Bag, The Phantom,* and, of course, *Buffy the Vampire Slayer*. In several interviews, the actress offers a few details on her portrayal of the young vampire slayer.

"Buffy is a girl, and Buffy kicks some hard ass, but it goes a little deeper than that," said Swanson. "It's not about, 'I'm a woman and I can kick anyone's ass.' It's about change and challenging yourself, getting over your fears and taking one step further. Buffy may walk into a dark room, but she's still afraid. Her biggest fear is, what are her friends going to think? In the beginning Buffy knows the price of everything and the value of nothing. She's so shallow. [She's] an eighteen-year-old senior with no value system in her life. At first, she doesn't want to be a Slayer, but then she sort of gets into it. She senses the vampires coming—she gets a cramp. My secret weapon is PMS.

"I enjoy characters," she added. "I learned to study people, family, friends, everybody. That was more important than going to the prom. My sister-in-law, Jyl, was the model for Buffy. I observed her for weeks before shooting because she had that attitude. No professor can teach you that.

"When I got the role, they never asked me if I was a fighter. I did have a dance background. I did flying kicks. It's a matter of making the moves big and dirty. Even before *Buffy* I was interested in martial arts and boxing. When I did *Buffy,* I trained for a couple of weeks and got to learn all the fighting moves I would use in *Buffy,* and then after *Buffy* I still stuck with it here and there, training with various different martial arts trainers."

In one interview, Swanson humorously suggested a sequel to *Buffy* that would co-star former *Beverly Hills 90210* heartthrob Luke Perry. "We thought it might be kind of funny if Buffy joined the cast of *90210*," she laughed. "Suddenly Buffy is chasing vampires around Beverly Hills High and starts running down the street and onto the set of *Melrose Place.*"

Unfortunately for the actress, Swanson was never given the chance to reprise the role.

Albert L. Ortega

RUTGER HAUER PORTRAYED THE LEADER
OF THE VAMPIRES IN THE FEATURE FILM.

"Joss said to me, 'Are you insane?' about doing both movies, but he's been totally behind it," Gellar enthused. "Obviously, he understands people's desire to do movies and that's how he started. Though he would like me to do a movie for him now, since I've done two Kevin Williamson films."

Returning for year two of *Buffy the Vampire Slayer* was a little different for Gellar than the show had been in year one, as the series had garnered something of a reputation for itself. "It feels like we're working now," she said. "It's about work and we have to maintain a certain level and I've been so busy

Back to the Future at the same time that he was filming *Family Ties,* and George Clooney went from *E.R.* to the *Batman and Robin* sets during the same period.

I have to go to work and then to my other work. But Joss is our little cheerleader and has made the show feel like family. Everyone's really supportive."

Year two of the series provided a variety of interesting developments for the characters, increasing romantic intrigue between Angel and Buffy while simultaneously creating a distance between Buffy and Xander since she's learned the depth of his feelings for her. "We're really delving into what it's like to be in love with someone you can't really be with," she noted. "Angel's a vampire, she's a Slayer. It's the typical Romeo and Juliet story." Which should become even more complicated, as there are rumors the WB will spin the Angel character off into his own show.

Currently, the biggest thing on Gellar's mind is the fatigue she is no doubt feeling from her nonstop schedule of the past two years. "After the films, the TV schedule seemed really hard on me," she mused. "There never seemed to be enough time. There never were enough takes. I didn't get the script far enough in advance. Then I thought, 'I used to be on a soap. I used to learn a script a day.' How quickly we forget. I have, however, been asking them for the coma episode. I've been working seven days a week for so long and haven't had a weekend off forever. I was doing the movies, then working the press junkets, doing photo shoots, and even some commercials. I'm not complaining, don't get me wrong. This is what I want to do. This is my life and it's all been happening so fast for me. So right now, I'm real tired and that coma episode couldn't come soon enough."

CHAPTER TWO

THE SUPPORTING CAST

NICHOLAS BRENDON
(Xander Harris)

In the opinion of actor Nicholas Brendon, God is using him as a tool of communication. On a metaphoric level, of course.

"Oh yeah, I'm Joss Whedon in high school," he laughed, referring to *Buffy the Vampire Slayer*'s creator and executive producer. "I think what Joss wanted is a situation where he can now completely manipulate and write the situation the way he sees fit. He plays God now. If he wants that girl, by golly, by going through me he's going to get that girl. He can say all the funny lines and have all the retorts quickly, very witty, and wry. I like that. I think he went to high school in Europe at an all boy's school, so it wasn't a typical high school situation. I think it made him even more insecure when he went out to the real world. We had that conversation, where he told me that Xander was him in high school."

Not that Brendon can't identify with the trials and tribulations of high school faced by both Whedon and Xander. "I was horribly insecure in high school," he recently noted. "I wanted to be funny but I had a stutter. One of the reasons I got into acting was because I have a stutter, and that's why I'm hard on myself when I act. I lived my whole childhood life and high school with a stutter that I couldn't control. It took a lot of hard work. When I want to do something a

ACTING WAS NOT BRENDON'S ORIGINAL VOCATION OF CHOICE. FOR MANY YEARS HE HAD HOPED THAT HE WOULD BECOME A PROFESSIONAL BASEBALL PLAYER. "I WANTED TO PLAY WITH THE DODGERS AND HELP THEM WIN A WORLD CHAMPIONSHIP. TRAGICALLY, GOD SAID NO," HE SAID.

ferring to an arm injury that played a part in shortchanging that dream. "So I went into acting. I was a great player but there are so many politics in baseball and you have to be really lucky and in the right place at the right time. It sounds similar to acting, but with acting I was really naïve. With baseball, I knew what had to be done so that would knock me down."

Brendon made his television debut in a Clearasil commercial, but a lack of work led him to take on the role of production assistant on the sitcom *Dave's World*. This led to a guest-starring role on the Harry Anderson series, and that in turn fired up his ambition and confidence to follow acting as a career. He began with a recurring role on the soap opera *The Young and the Restless*, and a pilot called *Secret*

certain way, it has to be that way otherwise I'll beat myself up for it."

Acting was not Brendon's original vocation of choice. For many years he had hoped that he would become a professional baseball player. "I wanted to play with the Dodgers and help them win a world championship. Tragically, God said no," he said, re-

Lives. He appeared in the film *Children of the Corn III: Urban Harvest,* and on stage in *The Further Adventures of Tom Sawyer, My Own Private Hollywood,* and *Out of Gas on Lover's Leap.* His big break, naturally, was being cast on *Buffy.*

"I think *The X-Files* opened the doors for this kind of show," he offered. "After a while you start thinking, 'When are the great scripts going to stop coming?' But they don't. I feel so fortunate to be doing such good material. As far as Xander is concerned, I would say in season two he became more assertive. There's still a tinge of insecurity, there's also love. I think the show is maturing. The cast has matured, the writing has matured, and we can take more chances with the

Albert L. Ortega

As Xander, Nicholas Brendon is the celluloid version of series creator Joss Whedon.

stories. For the first twelve we were kind of safe, but now we're accepted and we can do more of our own thing."

ALYSON HANNIGAN BEGAN HER CAREER IN ATLANTA, WHERE SHE STARTED SHOOTING COMMERCIALS, MOVING ON TO SUCH NATIONAL SPOTS AS MCDONALD'S, SIX FLAGS AMUSEMENT PARKS, AND OREO COOKIES. AT THE RIPE OLD AGE OF II, SHE MOVED TO LOS ANGELES WITH THE HOPE OF BREAKING INTO FILM AND TELEVISION.

ALYSON HANNIGAN
(Willow Rosenberg)

Before essaying the role of the shy Willow Rosenberg on *Buffy*, Alyson Hannigan began her career in Atlanta, where she started shooting commercials, moving on to such national spots as McDonald's, Six Flags Amusement Parks, and Oreo cookies. At the ripe old age of 11, she moved to Los Angeles with the hope of breaking into film and television.

"I moved out here to be near the acting," she explained, "because that's what I've always wanted to do since I was a little kid. I started commercials when I was four, and I've been doing it all of my life. It was an after school sort of thing. Some people would go off to ballet, I would go to a commercial shoot. Commercials are just a day here or a day there, and I didn't miss much school. And I loved it. I also had regular activities. I was on the soccer team, I was a kid. I just had a job that I loved. I've done features and I was on this sitcom a while ago, but *Buffy* is by far the best thing I've done. I did some movies of the week that were horrible, but they weren't the same thing as a horror series. I'm a fan of the genre, but such a wimp when I watch the movies because I will basically jump into the lap of the person next to me. But I love it."

Hannigan's break-through role was as Dan Ackroyd's daughter in *My Stepmother Is an Alien*. Guest-starring appearances followed on *Picket Fences, Roseanne,* and *Touched by an Angel*, then there was a recurring guest-starring role on *Almost Home* before becoming a series regular on *Free Spirit*. Most recently she co-starred in the MTV film, *Dead Man on Campus*.

Despite the fact that *Buffy the Vampire Slayer* deals quite extensively with the world of horror, the only aspect of the show that has frightened Hannigan has been her own performance.

Albert L. Ortega

ALYSON HANNIGAN IS SO MUCH MORE THAN A WALLFLOWER AS WILLOW.

"In episode twelve, 'Prophecy Girl'," she recalled, "there's this huge, enormous slimy monster attacking my leg. It's wrapped a tentacle around my leg and is pulling me. They gooped it up with this slime stuff. It's real disgusting and it's really scary and then they turn on these air things so they would flop around. And they were making this hissing sound, so I was genuinely screaming to myself at that point. And then I watched the footage and my hands were up here at my face and I looked so fake. It was like the fakest moment I've seen in this show that I've done, and yet it was so real. It was my natural reaction, but it looked really fake. Of course only I noticed it, because I'm so critical, but I thought, 'What a dork.'"

The actress believes that she most definitely influences her on-screen persona, Willow. "I definitely think I give her the positive outlook," she said. "I had a problem when I first got the audition and stuff, because it was basically kind of sad: she can't get a date, she's in love with this guy who doesn't know she really is a girl, and all of that stuff. But nobody wants to watch a character walk around saying, 'Oh, look at how sorry I feel for myself.' So to make her more positive, it's easier to like her.

She's okay with herself. That's what I like about her: she's positive even though she's in love with somebody she can't have."

DAVID BOREANAZ (Angel)

The success of the character of Angel—and his enormous popularity—is probably just as surprising to his real life alter ego, David Boreanaz, as it is to anyone else. A relative newcomer to Hollywood, the actor has been swept up in a media windstorm that has resulted in his getting a spin-off series of his own set to debut fall 1999.

"Things haven't changed drastically," Boreanaz recently explained in terms of the impact all of this has had on his life. "I'm still the same. I still wake up, shower, and come to work. I'm just happy to be working. While it's exciting to be recognized for the work, it's also exciting to be involved with such a great group of people."

A native of Philadelphia, Boreanaz was exposed to the television industry

[BOREANAZ] BEGAN HIS LIFE IN HOLLYWOOD BY PARKING CARS, PAINTING HOUSES, AND HANDING OUT TOWELS AT A SPORTS CLUB. AMAZINGLY, HE WAS "DISCOVERED" BY AN AGENT WHILE HE WAS WALKING HIS DOG.

while a child as his father was a veteran weather forecaster for WPVI in Philadelphia. Despite this, he first got the acting bug at the age of seven when he caught the Yul Brenner starrer, *The King and I.* After graduating from Ithaca College, he moved to Los Angeles, deciding to give Hollywood a shot.

Like many an aspiring actor, he began life in Hollywood by parking cars, painting houses, and handing out towels at a sports club. Amazingly, he was "discovered" by an agent while he was walking his dog. This led to a guest-starring appearance on *Married . . . With Children* and the TV movie, *Men Don't Lie.* He has graced the stage in *Hatful of Rain, Italian-American Reconciliation, Fool For Love,* and *Cowboy Mouth,* and the big screen in *Aspen Extreme, Best of the Best 2,* and *Eyes of the World.*

As far as Boreanaz is concerned, working on *Buffy* is a great gig, allowing him to work with wonderful material and delving into the area of horror, which he has always enjoyed.

"I've always liked horror films," he recently explained. "When I was a kid, *Frankenstein,* the original movie, scared the hell out of me. I've always been fascinated with the film *Nosferatu,* and when I saw the film the first time it was eerie. You have no choice but to get into the genre because you're surrounded by all these vampires and it's amazing when you

Albert L. Ortega

TORTURED WORKS: DAVID BOREANAZ
WILL BE GETTING HIS OWN SPIN-OFF SERIES.

wild. It's very cool. It's a lot of fun and it's a genre that Hollywood loves to portray. And the prosthetic part of playing the part isn't too bad. Angel changes only when he's confronted by evil vampires, so he's usually showing up regular faced. But when he does change, it's usually not that bad of a process. It's pretty quick. The only painful part is taking it off. It's tedious because you can't just peel the stuff off because you'll rip your skin. So you have to easily take oil and use brushes to take it off.

"The show itself," he closes, "is really well written and it just goes to show you that if you have the writing and the right chemistry between the cast, things really do work out for the best."

have all these extras in vampire makeup, or you're in the graveyard shooting and you look around and see vampires hanging out, it's pretty

CHARISMA CARPENTER
(Cordelia Chase)

On her way to becoming an English teacher, Charisma Carpenter somehow ended up becoming a actor.

Born in Las Vegas, Carpenter lived there until she was 15, when her family moved to Mexico and San Diego to takes classes at the School of the Creative and Performing Arts. After graduating from high school, she traveled through Europe. Upon returning, she moved to San Diego where she held various jobs to support herself through junior college. Her job experience at that time included working in a video store, teaching aerobics, and waiting on tables. In fact, Carpenter was waitressing in Los Angeles, hoping to save up enough money for her education when she was discovered by a commercial agent. She appeared in more than 20 commercials, including one for Secret antiperspirant which ran on television for two years.

Her first television acting role was a guest shot on an episode of *Baywatch,* which led to a costarring position in Aaron Spelling's short-lived NBC series, *Malibu Shores,* and that gig was followed by her being cast as Cordelia on *Buffy.*

CARPENTER WAS WAITRESSING IN LOS ANGELES, HOPING TO SAVE UP ENOUGH MONEY FOR HER EDUCATION WHEN SHE WAS DISCOVERED BY A COMMERCIAL AGENT. SHE APPEARED IN MORE THAN 20 COMMERCIALS, INCLUDING ONE FOR SECRET ANTIPERSPIRANT WHICH RAN ON TELEVISION FOR TWO YEARS.

Albert L. Ortega

CHARISMA CARPENTER TOOK WHAT COULD HAVE BEEN A NOTHING ROLE AND TURNED IT INTO A FLESH-AND-BLOOD HUMAN BEING.

"I was auditioning for *Buffy* while I was doing *Malibu Shores,*" she explained. "I guess they knew it was going to get cancelled soon. So I auditioned wearing overalls, a leather jacket, and flip flops. It was really a bizarre day. Joss Whedon was there and I didn't know that it was for producers only. I was actually reading for Buffy. Then they wanted me to read for Cordelia five minutes later. I did, and I guess they really liked it."

Carpenter was an immediate hit with the show's staff and with viewers, and in her capable hands Cordelia became an evolving character rather than a stereotypical high school bitch. "My character has changed from the beginning," noting that Cordelia is now working with Buffy and company to save Sunnydale from evil, though at the same time she always remains, at heart, true to herself. "She's always looking for attention and never getting it, and it's irritating to her. The fanmail is disheartening too, saying things like, 'Are you ever going to be nice?' My response is, 'I *am* nice. They're meaner to me than I am to them.'"

In her mind, season one wasn't very difficult, but year two was a different matter entirely. "Since I barely worked first season, I can't think of anything difficult," she offered. "But at the beginning of the second season, I was hung upside down on a meat hook by my feet. The pace that we're keeping this season, for me anyway, is much swifter than last season. I don't know if I was sick from nerves, but last season in my episode 'Out of Mind, Out of Sight,' toward the end I was throwing up. There was a scene with the invisible girl in the bathroom and it was a really convenient location because right after that scene was over I threw up three times. It must have been nerves or something. I'm adjusting again this season. The workload has been different. I'm always the victim, always in trouble. I asked Joss why I'm not more involved with the group when they're off digging up bodies, because I think there are potentially a lot of funny things that would come out of that. He said, 'We have to get you out there so you can be kidnapped and be the victim.'"

Carpenter is not only a fan of the material, but she's quick to praise her fellow cast members as well. "I think this cast is extremely intelligent, and I'm not trying to speak for myself," she detailed. "Sarah, for instance, has this maturity about her that is not conceivable at 20. You don't envision anyone at 20 having that kind of maturity. She carries a lot of pressure and weight on her shoulders, and she does it with professionalism and finesse. Alyson is really young and young-hearted and full of love, and really giddy and happy and witty. Nicky is just over the top. He also, when you get to know him, has a naïveté about him as well. He's very vulnerable and I think that's where his humor comes from. In working with these people, it's like I'm the audience because I can't keep up with them. They're all amazing."

ANTHONY STEWART HEAD
(Rupert Giles)

You probably know him best from those Taster's Choice commercials—you know, the romantic ones with the man and woman endlessly flirting with each other, yet both of them are obsessed over coffee. Yet there is so much more to actor Anthony Stewart Head.

He was a regular performer on Fox's sci-fi series *VR.5* and guest starred in such shows as *Highlander: The Series* and *NYPD Blue*. Additional credits include the Showtime movie *Royce* and the feature films *A Prayer for the Dying, Devil's Hill,* and *Lady Chatterly's Lover.*

Born in Camdentown, England, Head has performed in several BBC productions, including *Secret Army, Accident, Bergerac, The Grudge Fight, Howard's Way, Pulaski, Enemy at the Door,* and *Love in a Cold Climate.* His London stage appearances include *The Rocky Horror Picture Show, Julius Caesar, The Heiress, Chess, Yonadab,* and *Rope.*

Of portraying Buffy's Watcher, Rupert Giles, he noted to the press, "Giles knows so much about vampires and monsters, but he knows nothing about life. That's Giles. That's why it's interesting that he's suddenly talking about women [in season two]. Dealing with Buffy is one thing, because he starts off treating her like a child, but gradually realizes that that's a bad idea. It ain't a sexual thing, but all of a sudden he's got this other woman [Ms. Calendar] who's posing all of these difficult questions. She is Giles's antithesis and believes in everything he has complete contempt for, except that they have common ground. She understands where he's coming from, so they've always had that in mind. The relationship is interesting where he has to basically fulfill his role as a Watcher and not protect everyone else. It's very different from Donald Sutherland in the feature, but I think the whole premise has changed since then because Joss has brought out the fact that he [Giles] knows so little about life. He's a strange, bookish, learned person. Everything's academic, and the first time he confronts a vampire, it's a shock. It's one thing to read and learn about something, but quite different when you're actually confronting your fears.

"I find in life," he added, "that you shouldn't question anything. Everything happens for a reason and you find yourself in a position of saying, 'Why am I here?' but then you do understand, and it is for a reason. Giles finds himself in that position. I think his father was a Watcher before him. I don't think maybe he even wants to be a Watcher. I think in one episode he says he wanted to be a grocer or a fighter pilot, but he has to accept his destiny just as Buffy has to accept hers. What's nice, also, is that Joss has started to take our preconceptions and turn them on their heads. In fact, we all became comfortable in our lot in the last season and everything changes in year two. Our expectations change, and our

Albert L. Ortega

He's a hell of a Watcher— but does he still drink Taster's Choice?

roles change as much as suddenly I have someone else I care for, and therefore how does that affect me as a Watcher? Buffy's whole thing with Angel is throwing her into a situation of, 'How can I be a Slayer and be in love with a vampire?' Joss is just very clever with drawing the characters out and making them develop, rather than just getting comfortable and cozy with what we know they have. I was joking that no character is safe. Yeah, we've all got contracts but he could kill any of us, because he loves messing with people's minds. I thought it was wonderful when Principal Flutie was killed. At that moment, you knew there were no lines that couldn't be crossed. The guards were down. It's just nice to mess with people's minds. The other thing is that there's no such thing as a character dying off, because they can always come back.

"It really is a magical show," enthused Head. "Joss knows absolutely, without any shadow of a doubt—even to the point of how people are dressed and how people relate to each other—where he wants the show to go. That's really important, having someone with that much control and being that sure of what they're doing with that control. With *VR.5* we had a lot of producers. John Sacret Young, who had the overall

vision, was always getting messages from the network, 'We do like this, we don't like this, we want more of this.' Here it just feels like a tight ship. The network will comment on a few things, but they also let a lot of things go. Also, there is the fact that it started as an 8:00 slot in everybody's mind and has grown into what it should have always been. This has the widest demographic that I think any show has. It doesn't just reach teenage kids. It's the same thing that Joss did with *Toy Story*. It's not necessarily a kid's movie. Kids can get off on it and they can identify with it on that level, but there are lots of levels you can identify with that adults can enjoy. This show works on so many levels and it's about human relationships and what we all fear in ourselves and each other. It's largely a metaphor for life and that's cool."

JAMES MARSTERS (Spike)

As the male half of what series creator Joss Whedon calls "The Sid and Nancy of the vampire set," James Marsters has brought a vicious coolness to Sunnydale, and was a more than suitable successor to the show's Master character. Appearing both in films and on stage, Marsters attended Juliard and starred in such classics as *Twelfth Night* and *Troilus and Cressida*.

JULIET LANDAU (Drusilla)

If James Marsters is Sid, then Juliet Landau is most definitely Nancy, the psychic and psychotic vampire companion to Spike.

She began her career in Los Angeles and performed all over the world before returning to her home town. She attended the American School in London and graduated from the North Carolina Center for the Arts, starting her career as a ballerina. While she may have paid the bills dancing for five years, acting was always something that she was interested in. She joined the Actor's Studio and started auditioning. Her film roles include *The Grifters, Theodore Rex,* and *Ed Wood*.

"I love being bad," she said in an online interview regarding her character, Drusilla. "The fun thing about the character is also with James's character, we have a sweet relationship. Kinky but sweet, but there are things that balance out the evil deeds that we do. It's fun to be evil, but it's nice that she's well fleshed out, because there are other aspects. She plays with dolls, even though she stabs the dolls' eyes. For the first six episodes I was sort of on death's door, but then I got renewed power. So that was fun, to have that arc, from being very weak to strong.

"People talk about doing television and sort of getting stuck in a role," Landau added. "This role has had so many areas and so much growth that that's, I think, the biggest part. To me, that's what acting is about—it's the role and getting to do a full range of characters and a diversity, and this is definitely very different than any character I've done prior. In terms of being disciplined, there is nothing like being a ballerina for it. It's funny to me sometimes when I'm on the set, and you're working 16 hours and people

JULIET LANDAU PORTRAYS
THE VAMPIRESS DRUSILLA.

you for anything. That discipline makes you show up for work on time, makes you very organized, all of that stuff which is a definite plus. For me, a character's physical presence is very interesting; how you can tell so much about a person, how they walk into a room, how they carry themselves, what part of their body they're happy with or not happy with. That ability is a plus."

SETH GREEN (Oz)

He's just your typical, misunderstood werewolf.

According to his official press biography, Seth Green has been acting professionally since age six. By the time he was twelve, he had a leading role in the Woody Allen feature film, *Radio Days*.

are complaining. I think, 'My feet aren't bleeding. What are you complaining about?' You're used to such a rigorous lifestyle that it sort of prepares

Since then he has starred in numerous television and film projects, including *Austin Powers, The X-Files,* and *Stephen King's It.*

Green began his role as Oz in 1997. Joss Whedon told Green, "Oz would have the same reaction to spray cheese as to true love," says Green. "Oz is unflappable and I love being the guitar player on TV. I'm living out my rock and roll fantasy." Four episodes turned to five, then eight, and now it's endless. "The show is so fun and quirky, but there's a lot of heart to it, that's what's so appealing," describes Green. "It's smart, scary, and funny."

As for playing a werewolf, Green says, "They take their monsters pretty seriously without the show taking itself too seriously." And the transformation? "It takes a lot of time and it's really difficult to stand still," says Green. "It starts at 11:30 AM and goes until 4:30 PM. They have to hand lay all of the hair on me, but the make-up artists there are so great, so sweet and considerate. They make it as painless as possible and the end result is worth the effect."

What does Green do when he's not starring in film and television? "I read a ton of magazines, I play pool, I love to see any movie that's out, good or bad. The one bad thing about working," laments Green, "you can't watch all the movies."

ROBIA LA MORTE (Jenny Calendar)

According to her official biography, when Robia La Morte was first cast as Jenny Calendar, it was meant to be a one-time guest-starring role as a sexy computer teacher/cyber pagan. However, she turned more heads than expected, prompting Joss Whedon to keep her around Sunnydale, much to the pleasure of Buffy's mentor, librarian Rupert Giles. While the two try to keep their tryst discreet, none of the characters are fooled.

La Morte was interested in the arts from a young age and dedicated her life to making it in the competitive world of showbiz. She studied at the Los Angeles High School for the

Performing Arts and the Dupree Dance Academy.

Before she could drive, Robia was dancing professionally at 16 and was cast in several music videos. A few years later, she met a rock star who was then known as Prince and the two changed each other's lives. She inspired his famous "Diamond and Pearl" theme, and was the lead dancer and Prince's spokesperson during his self-imposed public silence. After leaving the wide weird world of Prince at age 22, La Morte tried her hand at acting.

She was cast on *Beverly Hills 90210* as the New York native Jill Fleming. Her work on the show led to guest-starring roles on *The Sentinel* and *Lawless* and supporting roles in the films *Earth Girls Are Easy* and *Spawn*. When asked what she thinks of her current role, La Morte is thrilled: "Jenny is such a great role. It's wonderful to play a character who is smart, sexy, and funny. It's the kind of role I've dreamed of since I first started my career."

CHAPTER THREE

WHEDON THE VAMPIRE CREATOR

When your writing is nominated for an Academy Award, what do you do for a follow-up? Well, most Hollywood screenwriters would parlay that success into a *major* feature film career. In the case of *Toy Story* scribe Joss Whedon, he shocked just about everyone by turning to television and the WB's *Buffy the Vampire Slayer,* which was based on the film that he'd provided the original script for.

Although Whedon's uncredited rewrites include *Speed* and *Waterworld* and although he fully scripted *Alien Resurrection,* he finds himself far more comfortable on the small screen. "In a way," he told *Cinescape* magazine, "I find that as I slowly become more successful as a writer, I have less power. Once you start making the big money and working on the big projects, you lose freedom. All of a sudden there are movie stars, producers, and a variety of people who are trying very hard to make the film work their way, and there's really no place for the writer. You may get to play in the big leagues, but you never actually get the ball. When they were filming *Alien Resurrection,* I was sure what was going on down on the set was pretty cool. But it's a totally different experience for me than this. The director does whatever he wants on a film. I see a lot of the scenes I wrote and I'm thinking, 'Well, it would have been better like this,' and I also see a lot of it realized just so beautifully. Ultimately, though, my heart is at *Buffy,* because my body is here. This is like making little movies on the sly. You have an idea and three weeks later you're prepping it, instead of waiting three years. I'm not ashamed to say that I like that. The bottom line is that I'm telling the stories I want to, which is something I've always dreamed about. There's nothing else on my resume that I can look at and say, 'That's pure me.'"

Whedon graduated from Connecticut's Westland College and moved to Los Angeles, where, like innumerable others, he began writing spec scripts. Apparently, luck was with him from the beginning, in that most spec writers never even get an opportunity to have their material read, yet Whedon abruptly found himself as a story editor on the former ABC sitcom *Roseanne* (a tour of duty he went AWOL from after one season).

"I liked the speed at which you had to turn something out on television," he related. "It taught discipline. In fact, at one point on *Roseanne* we fell behind and the plot of an episode was listed in *TV Guide* before we had written it. Deadlines really count in the medium. TV is tough, but it's all about the process. If it's good and you're turning out shows that are constantly good,

then it's worth it. But there are certain times when it's only about the personalities involved. It's about this guy's power and that guy's vanity, and all of a sudden all you're doing is turning out work. Toward the end of the year on *Roseanne,* that started to happen, which is why I quit. It was actually a lot of different factors, but basically the show started to suffer. It was all about who was angry at whom, and none of it was about, 'What should happen in next week's show?'"

Desiring to remove himself from the stress, Whedon segued over to NBC's short-lived adaptation of the Ron Howard film *Parenthood.* At the time, he was also writing the feature script *Buffy the Vampire Slayer,* a decidedly tongue-in-cheek affair in which a high school cheerleader is recruited to battle the undead. Although he was satisfied with his script, he was disappointed with the final results.

"What I started with was a horror action-comedy," he related to the press. "It had fright, it had camera movement, it had acting—all kinds of interesting things that weren't in the finished film. Apart from the jokes—and there had been a lot more of them, but all of my favorites were cut—it was supposed to have a little edge to it. It was supposed to be a visceral entertainment rather than a glorified sitcom where everybody stands in front of the camera, says their joke, and exits. I wasn't happy with anything about it, although there are people who are faithful to it. I had one advantage in that the direction was so bland that the jokes kind of stood out, because they were the only things to latch onto. But that was a big disappointment. It could have been a lot better."

Buffy was a box office failure, though it did eventually manage to score on videotape. Luckily for Whedon, his original script was well-known, and based on *that* rather than

APPARENTLY, LUCK WAS WITH [JOSS] FROM THE BEGINNING, IN THAT MOST SPEC WRITERS NEVER GET AN OPPORTUNITY TO HAVE THEIR MATERIAL READ, YET WHEDON ABRUPTLY FOUND HIMSELF AS A STORY EDITOR ON THE FORMER ABC SITCOM ROSEANNE (A TOUR OF DUTY HE WENT AWOL FROM AFTER ONE SEASON).

on the final movie, he secured plenty of work for himself as a script doctor.

"Basically, they call me when they are making a movie that they should not be making," he laughed. "It can be, 'God, this one scene doesn't work,' or it can be, 'Wow, this script sucks!' For me, it is connecting whatever dots they already have. It's taking everything

James Sorenson/Shooting Star

THE CAST OF <u>BUFFY THE VAMPIRE SLAYER</u>

that they're wedded to and trying to work something good in between the cracks. In the case of *Speed,* there was a lot of opportunity to do that. I couldn't change a single stunt, but I could change every word."

Along with a rewrite of most of the dialogue, Whedon felt that much of what he did for *Speed* wouldn't even be noticed by the audience. "I was trying to make the whole thing track logically and emotionally so that all of those insane, over-the-top stunts would make sense," he detailed. "That's the biggest part of the script-doctoring that I do. Somebody says, 'We've got a guy falling off of a cliff and later he's hanging off of a helicopter. We need you to tell us why. We need you to make the audience believe that he's doing it for a reason.' That's what *Speed* was about, apart from writing jokes and that kind of thing."

Even a script doctor is limited in the kind of miracles he can perform. For instance, Whedon spent six weeks working with Kevin Costner on *Waterworld*, but the end results were not nearly as fruitful as they had been on *Speed*. "The experience on *Waterworld* was pretty interesting," he told journalist Edward Gross. "By the time I got there, there was too much going on for me to make a real difference. They were too far into it. With *Speed*, I could really work on it. But with *Waterworld*, there were only tiny cracks that I could get

between. I'm not sure what kind of contribution I made."

He had far more influence on *Toy Story*, the computer-generated megahit from Disney in which toys from childhood are brought to life. Whedon admitted that he was thrilled to be involved and was extremely pleased with the final results. One mild disappointment, though, concerned some of the cuts that were made. "We kept putting stuff in there like Mr. Potatohead popping out one of his eyes so that it could roll under Bo Peep's dress and take a peek," he smiled. "I guess that was considered too risqué for the Disney board of directors."

At roughly the same time that *Buffy* was given a green light to make the transition to television, Whedon was given the gig of writing the fourth film in 20th Century-Fox's *Alien* series, *Alien Resurrection*. From the outset, it was no small challenge, given that "episode" three was generally perceived to be a failure and series heroine Ellen Ripley (Sigourney Weaver) committed suicide at the film's climax. Although it was a dream come true for the writer, the process of manifesting that dream was a long one.

"We had to work with the producers, we had to make the deal, we had to write a treatment, and here we are a couple of years later. But it's okay. I've been dreaming about this my whole life," he related. "I saw *Alien* when I was fourteen, and there's not another movie that's had as big an impact on me viscerally or aesthetically. *Alien* changed the nature of science fiction as much as *Star Wars* did by turning it into a working man's universe. It was a submarine movie. It was like that scene in *Star Wars* where Luke looks at the Millennium Falcon—which was the coolest thing I'd ever seen—and says, 'What a piece of junk!' Suddenly, you're no longer looking at guys in flowing robes, saying, 'Mars will explode!' Now science fiction is inhabited by you and me. That's part of the appeal, along with the fact, of course, that they created a monster that was not only genuinely new but also horribly resonant. That's what was disappointing about the third one for me. I thought the attitude and the feel were great, but people want to see something different. They say, 'We know the alien; we know it intimately. What's new? What's out there that's different?' When James Cameron made *Aliens,* he did that in spades just with the title alone. But then *Alien 3* said, 'Yeah, well, this one is small and kind of slow. Ooh, that's scary.'"

Of the last film, which was directed by David Fincher (*Seven, The Game*), Whedon noted to journalists, "It was beautiful to look at, but it was neither exciting nor scary, which is a travesty. So, yes, we might have to convince some people who didn't like *Alien 3* to see the new film. By the same token, you don't have a piece of genius to live up to. If the third one had been as great as the first two, I wouldn't go near this. I would be too frightened. I know what I wanted from a third *Alien,* and it wasn't a bunch of bald guys running around getting eaten. It was just a bitter, bleak movie. It's like the sequel to *Planet of the Apes,* where they nuked the Earth. I didn't feel that *Alien 3* was a step forward. A smaller, less ferocious alien was not what I imagined."

When developing the concept, Whedon realized that the previous entries in the series were based on other film genres, all of which have rules of their own: a submarine film, an army film, and a prison film. "Only *Alien 3* wasn't really a prison movie, and that's where it failed," he said. "A friend of mine said, 'Look at all the bald British guys, you can't tell one from the other.' That's not prison genre. In prison genre films they're all Americans, very specifically, and they actually had a scene where people we didn't know were killed by the alien. That's bullshit. That totally betrays these movies, because nothing is more boring and pointless than somebody you don't know anything about being killed."

One of the most highly circulated rumors surrounding the fourth *Alien* film was that it would be combined with Fox's other hoped for sci-fi franchise, *Predator*. Based on the Dark Horse comic of the same name, *Alien vs. Predator* at one point seemed likely to go into production. Whedon dismissed the notion of adapting it to film. "Some of us felt that might have sullied the *Alien* films," he said. "It becomes like *Destroy All Monsters*. You know, Godzilla, Rodan, Mothra, and all the rest. Or Freddy vs. Jason. Actually, I think the reason it fell through is that it was so unbelievably complicated legally. There are something like 19 producers involved, and I don't think they could do it. My opinion is that it would have been a mistake."

He also didn't agree with the other popular rumor: that the newest story should take place on earth. "First of all," he said, "it would require an enormous budget and gigantic scope, and I don't know if they're ready to make that commitment until they see if the series still has legs. Ultimately, it would have just been a backdrop that wouldn't affect the main part of the story or what the characters would be. What's interesting is that everybody thinks it would be a great idea, but what exactly about their coming to earth do you want? Nobody, including me, can answer that. We know the earth won't be anything we recognize, so it's not like you'd be afraid the aliens are under your bed. Ultimately, I

AT THE TIME, WHEDON WAS ALSO WRITING THE FEATURE SCRIPT <u>BUFFY THE VAMPIRE SLAYER</u>, A DECIDEDLY TONGUE-IN-CHEEK AFFAIR IN WHICH A HIGH SCHOOL CHEERLEADER IS RECRUITED TO BATTLE THE UN-DEAD. ALTHOUGH HE WAS SATISFIED WITH HIS SCRIPT, HE WAS DISAPPOINTED WITH THE FINAL RESULTS.

didn't know what we could extract from that idea, except a mankind versus the aliens epic, this all-out war kind of thing. I love finite space, and I think you need that in an *Alien* film. That's what James Cameron is so brilliant at, creating a space where you know everything you need to know and nothing else. What I wanted to create was a very specific space like that, instead of doing something so huge that it becomes vague. You know, here are our people and here is our problem. What I think you get from them coming to earth is the opposite."

Whedon discarded those possibilities and went back to the core of the franchise—Ellen Ripley—attempting to come up with a scenario that Weaver would approve. His first script treatment did not include the character, but apparently the notion of producing an *Alien* film without the actress proved too daunting a challenge to the studio. "I wrote a new treatment, and for a time I very jealously guarded the whole plot. It's like, 'Kirk dies.' Once something gets on the Internet, forget it," he mused. "But when they first suggested that we bring Ripley back, my reaction was, 'Bullshit.' But then I got so into it. Basically, once we figured out how to bring her back, I realized that there were a lot of interesting changes I could bring to the character."

Many of the changes came about due to the fact that in the film, Ripley is cloned from a blood sample taken back on the prison planet of *Alien 3,* for the purpose of extracting the hoped-for regenerated Alien Queen within her. "We dealt with Ripley's resurrection responsibly," said Whedon. "We weren't just saying, 'Oh, Sigourney's back, let's go make the movie.' It's the central issue of the movie, the fact that we bring her back. Once you do that, everything must be different. If somebody comes back from the dead, especially in a movie where death is the ultimate threat, you can't just say: 'It's okay, anybody can die and come back because we can do this now.' It's very important to me that it be a very torturous, sort of grotesque process so the audience can feel what it's like to be sort of horribly reborn in a lab. And Ripley's not too happy about being

brought back. She's angry and has to deal with a lot of shit. What's interesting for me is that she can be running a whole gamut of emotions. She can be amused when it's not funny, she can be all kinds of different people at this point—rather than just playing that same note again. I wanted to write a juicy part for Sigourney. I wanted her to have fun with it.

"I was looking at the first two movies as my templates," he continued elsewhere, "trying to find the suspense and the uncertainty about what we were going to see physically from the aliens in the first one, and the absolutely nonstop, 'I-can't-believe-this-is-still-going-on' action sequences of the second. But then I thought, 'No, actually, it just has to be a good yarn.' Actually, I was heavily into writing the movie before I realized I was being influenced by *The Poseidon Adventure.* You know, there is this group trying to get from one end of the ship to the other once the aliens have taken it over, so that basically it's the journey through the dark and into the woods, and the question is, 'What's next?' There's even an underwater sequence, the only difference being that in this underwater sequence they're not alone. There are some problems in the water and more problems when they get out. There are just problems, problems, problems. Structurally, that really helped me because once I understood that it was a journey, mythically, it made sense to me."

He was also influenced by Sam Raimi's *The Evil Dead.* "The first one, the great one, not the second one, the decent one," he said. "Everybody loves the second one. Yes, it's very funny, but the first one is the best. The first half hour is *scary.* Nothing is really happening, but you're waiting for the first terrible thing to happen. Thirty minutes into it, the first terrible thing happens and then all of these terrible things happen for an hour. There's no pause, no let-up. That, to me, was the idea. I wanted to set this up. I wanted to let the pieces fall into place. I wanted to play up the growing worry about what's going to happen with the aliens, and once the horror started, I didn't want it to stop until the closing credits.

There are pauses, there are scenes between, but basically the idea was just to keep the pressure on."

It obviously worked, as Weaver signed on enthusiastically. "I'm sure the gazillion-dollar paycheck had nothing to do with it," Whedon told journalist Edward Gross. "But she did seem to really respond to where I was going with the character and, based on her notes, she genuinely liked the script. She didn't come in with the attitude that she was slumming; she was totally into it, which is all you can ask for.

"The one scene I keep pointing to," he added, "is when the aliens escape and start killing everybody. Ripley's locked in her cell somewhere just laughing her head off. There's too much alien in her to get worked up over it. I wanted to have an edge to the character, a real moral and physiological ambiguity, and Sigourney just dove into it. She's playing more than bleak nihilism. She's very edgy in this one. That's what the whole movie is about. Who is Ripley? It's the question she's asking, and she has it answered in some

creepy and strange ways. Am I human? Do I care? How do I feel about the aliens? Everything is much more complex to her. That's really the essence of the movie."

And for the most part, it worked. *Alien Resurrection* was generally more positively received by critics and the audience than its immediate predecessor had been, but its final box office tally indicates that the franchise has gone as far as it possibly could. Insofar as Whedon is concerned, although he would undoubtedly love a crack at writing an *Alien 5,* his life at the time of the film's release and after that point has been completely wrapped up in the vampire slayings of young Buffy.

"BASICALLY THEY CALL ME WHEN THEY ARE MAKING A MOVIE THAT THEY SHOULD NOT BE MAKING. . . . IT CAN BE, 'GOD, THIS ONE SCENE DOESN'T WORK,' OR IT CAN BE, 'WOW, THIS SCRIPT SUCKS!' FOR ME, IT IS CONNECTING WHATEVER DOTS THEY ALREADY HAVE. IT'S TAKING EVERYTHING THAT THEY'RE WEDDED TO AND TRYING TO WORK SOMETHING GOOD IN BETWEEN THE CRACKS."

—JOSS WHEDON

Like the Fox network before it, the fledgling WB was definitely attempting to stake out the young audience that had all but abandoned ABC, NBC, and, especially, CBS. The idea was to come up with programming that had an edge, and *Buffy the Vampire Slayer,* despite its failure as a feature film, seemed ideally suited to its needs. For his first effort, Whedon couldn't have been happier, choosing to ignore the doomsayers who decried his shifting mediums.

"It makes sense to me," he has explained, "but it definitely surprises most people. But why are most of the best writers on TV? Because they can control their product; because they are given something resembling respect. Plus, it's steady work. That's my theory about why movies are usually so bad. Who in their right mind would want to write those? I love movies and I want to write more movies, but if the idea is to tell the story, then TV is the best way to do it. I also think that I've been helped by the fact that I don't really know what I'm doing. My ignorance works to my advantage. It's easy to break rules when you're not sure what they are. At the same time, I'm very traditional in telling a good story. I care about character and all that stuff. I'm actually a very conservative storyteller, and I think everyone on staff is completely dedicated. Our meetings are like, 'What is the emotional reality of being locked in a cage by the substitute teacher who turns into a giant praying mantis?' We're very curious about things like that, otherwise it becomes jokey. If you can't connect your

VAMPIRE MOVIES

Black Sunday (American International Pictures, 1960)

Bram Stoker's Dracula (Columbia, 1992)

Buffy the Vampire Slayer (20th-Century Fox, 1992)

Count Yorga, Vampire (American International Pictures, 1970)

Dracula (Universal, 1931)

Dracula: A Cinematic Scrapbook (Rhino Video, 1991)

Dracula's Daughter (Universal, 1936)

Fright Night (Columbia, 1985)

From Dusk Till Dawn (Dimension Films, A Band Apart, Los Hooligans, 1995)

Horror of Dracula (Hammer Films, Universal, 1958)

Innocent Blood (Warner Brothers, 1992)

Interview with the Vampire (Geffen Pictures, 1994)

The Lost Boys (Warner Brothers, 1987)

Mark of the Vampire (MGM, 1935)

Nosferatu (Prana, 1922)

story to some emotional reality, there's no reason to tell it."

In detailing his original conception for the premise, Whedon noted that in the mid-eighties he had grown tired of slasher film clichés, most notably the dumb, oversexed blonde stumbling into a dark place to have sex with a boyfriend, where, preferably in an advanced stage of undress, she's brutally murdered by Jason, Freddy, or one of their countless screen imitators. "I began thinking that I would love to see a scene where a ditsy blonde walks into a dark alley, a monster attacks her, and she kicks his ass," Whedon laughed. "After all those times the poor girl had sex and got herself killed for it, I just wanted her to be able to take care of herself. So I had this character long before I had the idea of using vampires. I wanted to create a special person who desperately wants to fit in but who has a higher calling. I decided to use vampires because I've always thought vampires were so cool.

"The movie is pretty different from what I originally intended," he emphasized. "I like horror, but the movie ended up being more of a straight-on comedy. While it is an absurd story, I wanted to go for the thrills, the chills, and the action. The movie wasn't as focused on that as I was. They lightened up the tone, and I always like things as dark as possible. In my original draft, there were severed heads and horrible stuff going on. Camp was never my intent. I can't really write camp, because it takes you away from the characters. I don't like laughing at people, I like laughing *with* them.

"I think the TV Buffy is more evolved than the one in the movie," Whedon continued. "The idea of the movie is that Buffy is someone who is completely ignorant of the world, who was never expected to be anything except pretty—she's nice but self-centered and vacuous. Ultimately, she has to learn about the world because she has to learn about vampires and such, and becomes more mature as a result. This Buffy is dealing with the same stuff, but she's already a 'Slayer' and has been one for a while. She's instinctively a hero, but at the same time she's going to be dealing with the pain

"IF SOMEBODY COMES BACK FROM THE DEAD, ESPECIALLY IN A MOVIE WHERE DEATH IS THE ULTIMATE THREAT, YOU CAN'T JUST SAY: 'IT'S OKAY, ANYBODY CAN DIE AND COME BACK BECAUSE WE CAN DO THIS NOW.' IT'S VERY IMPORTANT TO ME THAT IT BE A VERY TORTUROUS, SORT OF GROTESQUE PROCESS SO THE AUDIENCE CAN FEEL WHAT IT'S LIKE TO BE SORT OF HORRIBLY REBORN."

—JOSS WHEDON

accepts what she is. It's just a question of balancing her life as a Slayer and as a teenager."

In the pages of *SFX* magazine, Whedon explained, "[In the beginning], the real problem I had was that the network wanted another *Clueless.* The first thing that the studio talked to me about was a *Power Rangers* half-hour afternoon show for kids, and it evolved from that. Yet the more I got into it, the more adult-oriented the show became. The studio understood what we wanted to do and that it should appeal to grown-ups."

Interestingly, one of the strangest comparisons made regarding the show was to *The Mighty Morphin' Power Rangers,* in that both shows feature teens who lead double lives as normal kids and as

of adolescence. So her journey isn't quite the same. She's already empowered, she's just trying to deal with how that empowerment affects her. She secret saviors of humanity. "I don't think *Power Rangers* give a flying Wally about reality," he countered. "I think what's really fun about *Buffy* is that our characters are constantly dealing with that particular balance. The humor in this comes from Buffy thinking, 'I have a math test coming up *and* I have a giant insect attacking me, and I have to deal with both of those realities.' They are also the only ones who know what's really going on. There are terrible things happening all the time—kids are dropping like flies at Sunnydale High—but everyone else is a little oblivious to what's going on."

The TV version of Buffy focuses on young Buffy Summers (Sarah Michelle Gellar), a teenager who has moved with her mother to Sunnydale, California, following strange events that occurred at her previous school (implying a bit of continuity between the events of the film and the television series). Unfortunately, Sunnydale High is located right over a Hellmouth, which is the source of vampires, werewolves, and other ghoulies. In her battles as the chosen one of her generation,

Buffy is aided by her "Watcher," Rupert Giles (Anthony Head), and friends Willow (Alyson Hannigan) and Xander (Nicholas Brendon). Her enemy is the Master Vampire and his minions.

"I decided that in the series Buffy was already a Slayer, and she's moved to a new town, Sunnydale, after being kicked out of her old school because of starting fights with vampires. I came up with this idea that her new high school was built on an area called Boca Del Inferno, which roughly translates into Hellmouth. So every mystical occurrence and monster could happen and we wouldn't be just restricted to vampires. If it would have just been vampires, I'm not sure if we could have carried it off," Whedon explained at a press conference. "But when you added zombies and demons, I began to believe we'd have a series here. If you look at movies like *I Was a Teenage Werewolf,* you'll see this combination of teen angst and horror has been going on for a long time. We are not going to get terribly issue-oriented. We will deal with teen subjects, because that is where all the interesting stories come from. The horror and the stories have to come from the characters, their relationships, and their fears. Otherwise, it won't really be interesting. We've broadened the premise with different monsters, different problems, new characters, and stuff like that. There's an idea in the 'high school horror show' that could sustain an entire television show that goes for years. People need the big bad wolf. They need something to project their fears on to. There hasn't been that on television for a long time."

While many critics in the beginning accused *Buffy* of being just another in a long line of *X-Files* rip-offs, Whedon and his writing staff have chosen, instead, to offer a unique perspective that effortlessly manages to combine humor, action, and horror, while somehow addressing the overall high school experience.

"*Buffy* is the most manic-depressive show on television," Whedon told *Rolling Stone*. "It ping-pongs from, 'Oh, it's light 'n' fluffy to 'It's *Medea*.' The show's appeal is that it speaks so plainly to the high school experience, which is something you just don't really ever get over. Everything's bigger than life. In high school, my internal life was so huge and so dark and strange and overblown and dramatic, that this show seems kind of realistic. And we try to talk with teenagers, not to them. Teen shows seem to have fallen into two categories. Actually, *90210* falls into both of them, which are, 'We're obsessed with sex' and 'We're obsessed with issues.' It's like, 'Today, Donna has sex and Brandon learns that racism is bad.'"

Elsewhere, he added, "What's fun about the show is, we never know from scene to scene which way it's going to go. A scene that starts out very dramatically could end up quite funny, or something truly horrible could happen in it. It's not sort of, 'Oh, here's the funny part, here's the scary part.' We really never know what's going to be highlighted. The show inclines more toward the horror than the humor. It owes more to *The X-Files* than it does to *Sabrina*. I think the best stuff happens when we remember the sort of human relationships that people have that are really twisted and scary and sort of extend those in to horror stories, rather than have a monster show up. That's where the stuff really disturbs me, when it's somebody's parent or somebody's friend who is turning into something horrible, and it brings up issues that are real and, therefore, actually very scary. Then there's also death and maiming and all that good stuff . . . a high school, generally. Everything is so turgid when you're in high school, everything is so powerful, so dramatic. I don't think there is a time in life when you really feel that way except in high school. I've said, and I will say it until I'm in my grave, that high school is a horror movie and a soap opera, and I'm trying to capture that in the show. A lot of these stories are supposed to work as funhouse-mirror reflections of normal life, so that the werewolf story we've

THE IDEA WAS TO COME UP WITH PROGRAMMING THAT HAD AN EDGE, AND BUFFY THE VAMPIRE SLAYER, DESPITE ITS FAILURE AS A FEATURE FILM, SEEMED IDEALLY SUITED TO ITS NEEDS. FOR HIS FIRST EFFORT, WHEDON COULDN'T HAVE BEEN HAPPIER, CHOOSING TO IGNORE THE DOOMSAYERS WHO DECRIED HIS SHIFTING MEDIUMS.

posited, for example, is basically a puberty nightmare. We're facing a sort of almost absurdly huge and horrific extension of our own normal, everyday experience."

When attempting to find a niche for the show, the WB referred to it as *"Clueless Meets The X-Files,"* a moniker Whedon never really agreed with.

"*Clueless* is a bit of a misleading comparison only because that's really a camp TV show that laughs at people—everybody's sort of a joke," he said. "This is an actual hour drama where, although it's got a huge amount of humor, it takes itself seriously. It's not one of those post-modern things where everything is a big joke. I also don't think that it's visually as dark as *The X-Files.* There's a lighter side to the show, and not everyone is Canadian. But I guess that's the closest forbear. It's very plot driven, dealing with what the characters are facing and how they deal with it. When the WB said, 'Do you want to do the show?' I went a little more toward the horror because that's more my bent. But, truthfully, comedy and horror are more compatible than action and horror because both are about not being in control of your environment.

"A lot of great comedy comes from a character's lack of control: not knowing what's coming out of the frame. Not just in terms of slapstick, but in the case of something like *Groundhog Day*—the guy is out of control of his environment and is just completely confused by what the hell is going on. A horror movie is sort of the same thing. What the hell is going on? Except that the guy has a really big axe or it's a slimy monster. In a horror movie it's very much about, 'I don't understand the space that I'm in and I don't have control of the situation.' An action movie is, I have control of the situation and I understand the space I'm in. Action in the hands of someone like James Cameron—the man—the thing about his action is he tells you exactly what the space is, what the problem is, where the people are, what you need to do, and what's going to happen, and then uses that space. So you know exactly where everybody is. What's exciting is seeing your person control the space that they're in. That, to me, is textbook great action. Horror is the opposite. I go on about this because it's the hardest thing about *Buffy,* the show. You have to put a hero and character and her friends into peril, and at some point she has to take control and become an action hero, so we play both things. One of the things we're always saying is, 'We need a space that's small and dark enough for her to be scared in, but big and bad enough for her to kick ass in and us to get that epic sense that she's an action hero.' But I do think you can do both, and that's what we're really trying to do on this show."

Although readily admitting that the schedule of weekly television tends to burn him out, Whedon nonetheless refuses to allow the pressure to get to him.

"We do have fun with the show, and I honestly believe we have a good vibe on the set," he told *Movie Aliens* magazine. "I couldn't take the pressure of episodic television if the environment wasn't right. Is art worth pain? Yes, it is. Is it worth *me* feeling pain? Yes, it is. Is it worth me *causing* pain? No. That doesn't

BUFFY BOOKS

Cover, Arthur Byron. *Night of the Living Rerun.* New York: Archway, 1998.

Cusick, Richie Tankersley. *Buffy the Vampire Slayer.* New York: Pocket Books, 1997.

Cusick, Richie Tankersley. *The Harvest.* New York: Archway, 1997.

Golden, Christopher, and Nancy Holder. *Halloween Rain.* New York: Archway, 1997.

Holder, Nancy. *The Angel Chronicles.* New York: Archway, 1998.

Vornholt, John. *Coyote Moon.* New York: Archway, 1998.

ANNE RICE BOOKS

Rice, Anne. *Interview with the Vampire.* New York: Knopf, 1976.

————. *The Vampire Lestat.* New York: Knopf, 1985.

————. *The Queen of the Damned.* New York: Knopf, 1988.

————. *The Tale of the Body Thief.* New York: Knopf, 1992.

————. *Memnoch the Devil.* New York: Random House, 1995.

————. *Pandora: New Tales of Vampires.* New York: Knopf, 1998.

Rice, Anne, Faye Perozich, and Daerick Gross. *Anne Rice's Vampire Lestat: A Graphic Novel.* New York: Ballantine, 1991.

OTHER VAMPIRE BOOKS

Collins, Nancy A. *A Dozen Black Roses.* Palo Alto, CA: White Wolf Publishing, 1996.

King, Stephen. *Salem's Lot.* New York: Doubleday, 1990.

MacDonald, D. L., Kathleen Scherf, and John W. Polidori. *The Vampyre and Ernestus Berchtold; Or, the Modern Oedipus: Collected Fiction of John William Polidori.* Toronto: University of Toronto Press, 1994.

Matheson, Richard. *I Am Legend.* New York: Tor Books, 1997 Reprint Edition.

McNally, Raymond T., and Radu R. Florescu. *In Search of Dracula: The History of Dracula and Vampires.* Boston: Houghton Mifflin, 1994.

Stoker, Bram. *Dracula.* New York: Tor Books, 1997 Reprint Edition.

mean I'm always nice to everybody. I just try not to be a dick. Some days there is so much to do that I want to crawl into a womb. Everybody wants answers from me about a thousand different things. So sometimes, someone will ask, 'So what prop should we use?' and I'll freak out, 'Why do we have to have props? What ever happened to mime? Mime is a great art!' During those times everybody's like, 'Whoa, PMS on the Joss-man.' But I get over it. Fortunately, the writing staff that I've got is the best you could want. Great stories, never cheap, never bullshit, never how can we vamp until the end. In the end, if it comes down to my talking to the prop guy, we know there's a reason for it. When I directed the season finale of season one and the first episode of season two, it was such an extraordinary atmosphere. Every grip in there was busting his ass—I think be-cause they feel they're working on something worthwhile. I said, 'It's so great, everybody's working so hard.' It's because they care about it. That applies to us and everyone involved. If we don't love what we're putting on the screen, it ain't worth doing."

Unlike most executive producers, Whedon has also felt the full support of the network he works for. "The WB really let me get away with murder," he said. "They get what the show is, how strange it is, how all over the place and how sometimes edgy it is. We've never had a story thrown out or a real disaster. Sure, we've had standards and practices arguing, 'You've got to trim this or that,' so we go back and forth. That happens on every show. But they do get what we're do-ing and that's rare."

The same words can be applied to *Buffy the Vampire Slayer.*

CHAPTER FOUR

BUFFY THE VAMPIRE SLAYER

Episode Guide

SEASON ONE
Cast

Sarah Michelle Gellar
(Buffy Summers)

Nicholas Brendon
(Xander Harris)

Alyson Hannigan
(Willow Rosenberg)

Charisma Carpenter
(Cordelia Chase)

Anthony Stewart Head
(Rupert Giles)

Crew

EXECUTIVE PRODUCERS
Joss Whedon
Sandy Gallin
Gail Berman
Fran Rubel Kuzui
Kaz Kuzui

CO-EXECUTIVE PRODUCER
David Greenwalt

CO-PRODUCER
David Solomon

CREATED BY
Joss Whedon

PRODUCER
Gareth Davies

STORY EDITORS
Matt Kiene, Joe Reinkemeyer,
Rob Des Hotel, Dean Batali

PRODUCTION DESIGNER
Steve Hardie

DIRECTOR OF PHOTOGRAPHY
Michael Gershman

SCORE BY
Walter Murphy

THEME BY
Nerf Herder

Episodes One and Two: "Welcome to Hellmouth," "The Harvest"

Original Airdate: 3/10/97
Part One Credits:
Written by Joss Whedon
Directed by Charles Martin Smith
Guest Starring Mark Metcalf (The Master),
Brian Thompson (Luke), David Boreanaz
(Angel), Ken Lerner (Principal Flutie),
Kristine Sutherland (Mom), Julie Benz
(Darla), Eric Balfour (Jesse)

PRESS SYNOPSIS   Teenage vampire slayer Buffy Summers moves to a new town to make a fresh start but finds that her powers are sorely needed there. As Buffy tries to settle into her new surroundings, she is called upon to stop the Master Vampire from destroying the earth.

COMMENTARY (✝✝✝)   The first scene of the TV version of *Buffy the Vampire Slayer* quickly establishes the show's cinematic ties in terms of its creator, Joss Whedon.

A pair of teenagers break into Sunnydale High to head for the roof and some privacy; the young lady seems kind of nervous that they will be caught. When her date reassures her that no one will ever know they're in the building, she relaxes . . . then flashes her fangs and sinks them into his throat. It's very much a movie moment and, in fact, is somewhat reminiscent of the early seventies film *Count Yorga: Vampire,* the conclusion of which had a male and a female surviving the count's attacks and feeling they were safe, when one of them (unfortunately, I can't remember which) bares fangs and chomps down.

From the outset, things are treated more realistically than they were in the movie. Little more than a wink is given to Buffy's past as a Slayer. In addition, Sarah Michelle Gellar effortlessly manages to make the role of Buffy her own and makes the viewer forget Kristy Swanson's cinematic portrayal of the character. There's also a nice bit of character growth in terms of Buffy's negative reaction to the whole Valley Girl persona—showing that she has grown beyond that. At the same time, Buffy makes an interesting at-tempt to deny what she is—again, a bit of continuity with the movie—although it's inevitable that she ultimately embrace that destiny (otherwise, the show's over before it begins).

Gellar is in good company with Alyson Hannigan, who gives a touching portrayal of Willow Rosenberg, the wallflower desperately trying to break out of her shell. In many ways, Willow epitomizes the high school experience for many of the viewers. Nicholas Brendon is fine as Xander Harris, though he's a little tougher to get a handle on in this first episode. Anthony Stewart Head (that guy from the Taster's Choice commercials and the short-lived sci-fi series *VR.5*) replaces Donald Sutherland as Buffy's Watcher (Rupert Giles), and while he seems a bit stiff here, the potential definitely exists for a developing mentor/student relationship between him and Buffy.

Look for Brian Thompson—the Alien Bounty Hunter from *The X-Files* and a vampire in the Fox television series *The Kindred*—doing his usual villainy shtick as Luke, lieutenant to the

Albert L. Ortega

BUFFY AND THE SLAYETTES
AT THE MUSEUM OF TELEVISION AND RADIO.

"Master" vampire. There's also David Boreanaz as Angel, an enigma who, at this stage of the game, is either an ally for Buffy or a manipulator.

This episode establishes that Sunnydale High is built over a "Hellmouth," nicely laying out future possibilities for the series and moving

Buffy's slaying adventures way beyond the milieu of just vampires.

Part Two Credits:
Written by Joss Whedon
Directed by John T. Kretchmer
Guest Starring Mark Metcalf (The Master),
    Brian Thompson (Luke), David Boreanaz
    (Angel), Ken Lerner (Principal Flutie),
    Kristine Sutherland (Mom), Julie Benz
    (Darla), Eric Balfour (Jesse)

COMMENTARY (✝✝✝) One of the first things to strike you about the show is how humorous it is for pretty little Sarah Michelle Gellar to kick so much ass. She's a fairly petite package, yet not much can stand in her way

The episode opens as Giles is discussing demons with Buffy, Xander, and Willow. Essentially, they are addressing what seems, on the surface, to be an insane idea: they establish that the whole concept of a Hellmouth *is* ludicrous but then must accept what they saw in the previous episode as fact. It's refreshing and certainly different from most shows, in which everyone but the hero usually remains skep-

tical about strange events that occur, including the bodies that are piling up around them.

We're also provided with an inside look at the high-wire act Buffy has to perform on a daily basis. At one point, Principal Flutie (Ken Lerner) catches her on her way to slay vampires; he warns her not to leave the school grounds until the end of the school day (naturally, she leaps the gate when he's not looking). A similar scenario takes place later between Buffy and her mother, who, in an attempt to stop her daughter from getting into the same kind of trouble that resulted in her being kicked out of her last school, forbids her from going out. "Mom, it's a matter of life and death," she says sincerely. Mom responds, "When you're sixteen, everything's a matter of life and death."

David Boreanaz's Angel comes across as a bit of a cocky wiseass, but a real moment of pathos is evident when Buffy asks him, "Do you know what it's like to have a friend?" and he is perplexed by the question.

Anthony Head's Giles seems to be loosening up a bit, showing flashes of self-deprecating humor. Eric Balfour is effectively cast as the gang's friend, Jesse. From the beginning, we have the impression that he'll be a series regular. Even when he's captured by the vampires, we assume that it will only be a matter of time before Buffy rescues him. Instead, we're jolted out of our comfort zone by his being transformed into a vampire, ultimately meeting his end by the hand of his best friend, Xander.

Charisma Carpenter continues her role as Valley Girl Cordelia Chase, a beautiful but vacuous witch (not of the supernatural kind). Next to Tori Spelling, it would be hard to find anyone else you'd rather see killed by vampires than Cordelia.

This series has a cinematic feel and relies on editing more than most shows do (not, however, by using the jerky camera shots of *NYPD Blue* or the repeat cuts of *Homicide*).

A humorous scene reveals the secret compartment in Buffy's hope chest that contains stakes, holy water, and crosses.

The climax of the show, which takes place in a popular night club, is a vampire blow-up that is everything the *Buffy* movie finale should have been but wasn't. There is effective intercutting between the club and the vampires claiming victims, and the Master, who is gaining strength in the Underworld from each killing, getting closer to being able to unleash himself on the world. While the stunt work is first-rate, the battle between Buffy and Luke (Brian Thompson) is marred because there's no intercutting between that scene and the crowd of kids who have been established as standing before them. As a result, a great opportunity to heighten tension is lost. All in all, though, "Welcome to Hellmouth" and "The Harvest" set things up nicely and wash away the taste of the feature film.

Episode Three: "The Witch"

Original Airdate: 3/17/97
Written by Dana Reston
Directed by Stephen Cragg
Guest Starring Kristine Sutherland (Mom), Elizabeth Anne Allen (Amy), Robin Riker (Catherine)

PRESS SYNOPSIS An unpopular student's obsession with becoming a cheerleader is questioned when members of the squad start having unexplainable accidents.

COMMENTARY (✝✝✝) Buffy aims for a little normalcy in her life by trying out for the Sunnydale High cheerleading squad, but, naturally, things go awry.

The notion of parents living vicariously through their children is a sad fact (I see it all the time on my kids' basketball and soccer teams, where parents berate their children for not playing the way *they* would if they could). This episode, though, takes the idea to a whole new level. In many ways, the episode is like a twisted version of Disney's *Freaky Friday* or, to a lesser degree, the Tom Hanks vehicle, *Big*. The difference is that those efforts explored the fantasy of either being an adult or the opportunity to be young again, while "The Witch" is a more malevolent take on the material, fully exploiting the popular teenage battle-cry "You're trying to take over my

life." To have a mother, via witchcraft, doing just that to her own daughter, is pretty heady stuff and seemingly perfect for the realm of *Buffy.*

As the first non-vampire episode of the series, this particular show ran the same risk that the *X-Files* did when it presented its first non-UFO/government conspiracy episode. While this is certainly no "Squeeze," it nonetheless successfully opens the door for different types of terrors.

Many nice character moments occur in the show. Buffy reaches out to her mother in an effort to be closer to her, but mom claims that she doesn't have the time to do so. There are poignant moments as we learn that Buffy's parents have split up, which explains why there's no Mr. Slayer around. The episode also sets up the Willow/Xander/Buffy triangle—Willow is seriously in love with Xander, who has fallen for Buffy, who sees him as just a friend (while under a spell, she admits that she's "comfy" with Xander, thinking of him as one of the girls). Xander, in turn, is oblivious to Willow's feelings for him. While this could be completely clichéd, it's handled in a subtle enough fashion that it works, laying the groundwork for future episodes.

The scenes between Amy (Anne Allen) and her mother, Catherine (Robin Riker), have a certain spooky quality, with mom virtually cowering as her daughter approaches her.

Dopey point: When Giles is performing a chant to reverse the spell between Amy and her mother, why didn't anyone take the precautionary step of tying up mom, knowing that if the chant worked, the psychotic persona would return to the adult body?

There is a great final moment when mom's soul is transferred to a cheerleader trophy at Sunnydale, a fate she intended for Buffy until our Slayer pulled a mirror down and shot the "blast" back at the woman. This is a truly horrific punishment but one that scores high on the cool-concept meter.

Episode Four: "Teacher's Pet"

Original Airdate: 3/25/97
Written by David Greenwalt

Directed by Bruce Seth Green
Guest Starring David Boreanaz (Angel), Ken Lerner (Principal Flutie), Musetta Vander (Natalie French), Jackson Price, Jean Speegle Howard

PRESS SYNOPSIS A substitute teacher's infatuation with Xander is flattering to the lovesick teen but alarming to Buffy.

COMMENTARY (✝✝) Once again, a popular school fantasy—having a crush on your teacher—is given the *Buffy* twist and made considerably darker in the process, as the substitute teacher mentioned above, Ms. French (Musetta Vander), is actually a giant praying mantis, who morphs into human form so she can mate with virgins, have them fertilize her eggs, and then decapitate them. Unfortunately, Xander is one of her chosen targets.

There's a cute opening sequence in which Buffy is actually getting her butt kicked by a vampire, until Xander steps in and quickly dispatches him. It turns out to only be Xander's daydream, but it still represents a nice twist on the prince rescuing the damsel in distress theme.

This may be a sexist observation, but it seems that particularly in this episode Buffy's shirts are getting tighter and tighter, accentuating her natural charms.

There's a nice touch when Buffy's original biology teacher turns out to be one of the few people who is willing to forget about her past; it's just a shame he doesn't stick around long enough to prove the point, as he's one of the Mantis's first victims.

The enigmatic Angel (David Boreanaz) returns, doing his impersonation of *The X-Files*'s Deep Throat mixed in with a bit of classic Luke Perry/*Beverly Hills 90210* moodiness and angst.

In a bizarre scene, a vampire who attacks Buffy comes up against the Mantis in human form, seems to get frightened, and returns to the sewers. Here, we can see the influence of *Dark Shadows* on the show: myriad supernatural beings encounter each other and think nothing of it.

When Ms. French invites Xander over to her house one evening, Buffy tries to warn him, but Xander dismisses it as jealousy (as if!), simultaneously expressing his own heartburn over Angel. Later, Xander comes right out and admits to Willow that he loves Buffy.

While the idea behind the episode is pretty cool, the Mantis itself is kind of goofy-looking and, because of that, the final battle between Buffy and the giant insect takes place mostly in the shadows. As a result, the impact of the scene is badly diluted.

Dopey moment #1: Buffy finds her missing teacher's glasses on the floor of the classroom—it's days later and no one has cleaned this room since his disappearance? The police have checked it out? Not likely. An annoying red herring.

Dopey moment #2: In the middle of a classroom filled with kids taking a test, Ms. French twists her head 180 degrees so she can look at Buffy through the door to the classroom. What's the logic of having her do that, beyond showcasing a fairly neat special effect?

Dopey moment #3: The vampire who acted scared of Mantis Lady is captured by Buffy, his hands are tied behind his back, and she forces him to lead her to Ms. French's house. This scene totally lacks credibility.

Dopey moment #4: At the episode's conclusion, the dead teacher's glasses are *still* just sitting around, even after a new teacher has taken over the classroom. Even worse, the lab closet—which, apparently, no one ever bothers with—contains Mantis eggs that look like they've hatched. Again, how clueless can these people be?

Episode Five: "Never Kill a Boy on the First Date"

Original Airdate: 3/31/97
Written by Rob Des Hotel and Dean Batali
Directed by David Semel
Guest Starring Mark Metcalf (The Master),
    David Boreanaz (Angel), Christopher
    Wiehl (Owen), Geoff Meed (False
    Anointed One)

PRESS SYNOPSIS Buffy has her first Slayer/teenager dilemma when she must decide between stopping the forces of evil and going out with a handsome, poetry-loving classmate.

COMMENTARY (✝½) "Never Kill a Boy on a First Date" shares a certain kinship with the feature film *Superman II,* in that Buffy, like the Man of Steel, decides to pursue romance in her personal life, not realizing the price that others around her, and the world at large, come close to paying.

The object of Buffy's affection in this episode is Owen, who wanders into the library one day looking for Emily Dickinson but instead finds Buffy. Actually, this is the first time we've seen anyone other than Buffy, Xander, and Willow join Giles in the library—a novelty that is addressed when Owen first walks in and Giles says, "What do you want?" Buffy, perhaps giving the audience a bit of a wink, responds, "We're in a school. . . . This is a library."

Buffy's ensuing dilemma has her torn between her desire for a date and Giles's calculations that this particular night will mark the arrival of the Master's "Anointed One," born out of the ashes of five who die together—the

Anointed One being the person who can allow passage for the Master from one dimension to the other. Giles's calculations, surprisingly, turn out to be wrong, until there is an extremely well-staged bus crash claiming five victims, among them a child and a religious zealot named Zachery.

Too bad we've never seen Owen before, because Buffy's fascination with him seems unrealistic, particularly since we've been watching her feelings for Angel grow.

As the first non-vampire episode of the series, this particular show ran the same risk that The X-Files did when it presented its first non-UFO/government conspiracy episode. While "The Witch" is certainly no "Squeeze," it nonetheless successfully opens the door for different types of terrors.

Much of the episode deals with some conflict between Buffy and Giles regarding her feeling that she absolutely must go on this date. On the one hand, her obsession with her date with Owen seems inconsequential in comparison to the bigger issues, but, on the other hand, one has to remember that she *is* a teenager, with all the baggage that goes along with that condition. Unfortunately, this desire for personal happiness allows her to go out with Owen while Giles visits the Sunnydale Funeral Home to investigate the five deaths he's read about, in an attempt to see whether they are in any way connected to the Anointed One. Things get dopey at this point, as

Angel mysteriously shows up at the Bronze nightclub to let Buffy know that some serious crap is going down (but serving little more purpose than to raise the jealousy of both Owen and Xander). Once Buffy is made to realize what's going on, she takes forever to get to the funeral home where all the action is taking place.

Quite frankly, this is the point where the episode falls completely flat. Before cutting to the scene at the club, we see Giles threatened by vampires, and there's absolutely no way, with all the time that has lapsed, that the vampires threatening Giles could not have gotten their claws on him. His hiding on a body on a slab makes no sense, in that the vampires' inability to find him despite their superior senses proves them to be nothing more than fanged morons.

Buffy's arrival coincides with the resurrection of Zachery as a vampire. Unfortunately, Zachery's fate is similar to Owen's: since we never really got to know him beyond his being a repulsive zealot, his return doesn't mean that much to us. And his death at Buffy's hands—being hurled into a crematorium—is telegraphed so far in advance that absolutely no excitement is generated at all.

At the episode's conclusion, we're supposed to feel for Buffy when Owen tells her that he enjoyed the rush of the night before and wants to relive it, yet she has no interest because her life already has more excitement than she can handle. Frankly, the whole exchange registers as false. There's a great tag, though, where we learn that Zachery was *not* the Anointed One—that it was the child, instead, and that the young boy will now be tutored by the Master. A very creepy and well-done moment.

Incidentally, check out an opening battle between Buffy and a vampire, where the sound effects—legs whipping through the air, blows connecting—sound like something out of a classic kung fu movie. There's also another interesting part of the opening, in which the Master offers a rousing speech to his minions that he concludes by killing one of the more corrupt vampires among them. At the same time he notes, "Here endeth the lesson." One can only imagine that Hell, or wherever this Underworld is, has access to cable and the Master caught a run of Brian DePalma's *The Untouchables.*

Episode Six: "The Pack"

Original Airdate: 4/7/97
Written by Matt Kiene and Joe Reinkemeyer
Directed by Bruce Seth Green
Guest Starring Ken Lerner (Principal Flutie), Eion Bailey (Kyle), Michael McRaine, Brian Gross (Tor), Jennifer Sky, Jeff Maynard (Lance), James Stephens

PRESS SYNOPSIS A school trip to the zoo inexplicably turns Sunnydale's cool crowd into a bunch of savages.

COMMENTARY (✝✝✝) Bullies—particularly a gang of them—were yet another nightmare from the high school years for the less . . . aggressive . . . among us. "The Pack" exploits that notion to the utmost, as a group of punks (plus Xander) are possessed by the spirits of demonic hyenas.

It quickly becomes clear in this episode that Xander seems incapable of staying out of trouble; he comes across like Jimmy Olsen to Buffy's Superman. In "Teacher's Pet," he was the one who was nearly decapitated by a giant Praying Mantis, and in this episode he's the member of the show's triumvirate who is possessed by hyenas.

A nice character moment: Willow confides that Xander drives her crazy, while Buffy finally admits that she thinks Angel is a "honey," at least when he's not warning her about something and disappearing soon afterward.

Nicholas Brendon does a darker turn in this episode after he's possessed by the hyenas. His mannerisms and his facial expression really do take on a whole different countenance, and it's a terrific acting performance. In fact, his coldness results in a heart-wrenching moment when the possessed Xander tells Willow that he's dropping geometry, therefore he won't have to look at her "pasty face" any more. It's a truly painful scene, and Alyson Hannigan makes the moment extremely real.

There's an effectively staged scene in which Principal Flutie (Ken Lerner) threatens the pack (Xander's not with them) and orders them into his office. Many a time we may have wondered how a teacher or principal would deal with a group of students who completely reject authority. Well, in this case Flutie is literally eaten for his troubles. Although the scene is set up well, it's a shame that there's no emotional resonance over his death, because the principal was such a caricature to begin with that no one could possibly take him seriously.

There are a couple of really good moments, such as when the pack threatens a woman and her infant, but, thankfully, she gets away. Then there's the scene in which Xander, after being knocked out by Buffy and placed in a lab cage, attempts to manipulate Willow into letting him free—his effort, by the way, is unsuccessful.

More manipulation goes on as a zoologist tells Giles and Buffy to get the pack back to the zoo where the hyenas possessed them in the first place, so he can reverse what happened. In an un-expected plot twist, the zoologist plans to have the hyena souls transferred from the pack into himself, thereby accumulating incredible power. Unfortunately, the staging of the episode's conclusion is pretty anticlimactic, given the build-up and the excitement of Buffy being chased by the pack. Everything just seems to happen too easily; plus, the final battle between Buffy and the now empowered zoologist is over way too fast, when he is thrown into the hyena cage and torn apart.

Dopey moment #1: Buffy sees how the pack rips open a steel cage so that they can devour the school mascot—a pig—yet she places the possessed Xander in a similar cage after she's knocked him out. Although he doesn't actually escape, she should have realized that the same thing could have happened.

Dopey moment #2: Buffy and Giles are told by the zoologist that the pack will come looking for their missing member—Xander. Truthfully, there's no logical reason for Xander not to be with them in the first place, particularly after such a big deal is made about the pack doing everything together.

All in all, it is a strong episode that is made even more memorable by Brendon's aforementioned performance; he goes into realms as an actor that he has not equaled in subsequent episodes.

Episode Seven: "Angel"

Original Airdate: 4/14/97
Written by David Greenwalt
Directed by Scott Brazil
Guest Starring Mark Metcalf (The Master),
   David Boreanaz (Angel), Kristine Suther-
   land (Mom), Julie Benz (Darla)

PRESS SYNOPSIS Buffy is attracted to a mysterious stranger whose ancient history has Giles worried.

COMMENTARY (✝✝✝✝) In most television shows, there is an episode— usually pretty early in its run—where all of the elements come together creatively and say, in essence, "*This* is what our show is capable of achieving." On *Star Trek: The Next Generation* it was "Where No One Has Gone Before" and on *The X-Files* it was "Ice." For *Buffy the Vampire Slayer*, it is undoubtedly "Angel." The focus is on character and there's a wonderful line of tension throughout the show. Sarah Michelle Gellar, in particular, is a standout, humorous but always maintaining a sense of reality.

Things get off to a rousing start as Buffy goes up against "The Three," a trio of vampires dressed in Klingon-like regalia. It's a well-edited, suspenseful struggle in which we actually fear a bit for Buffy's survival (well, at least for a second or two), until Angel arrives and saves her. In the aftermath of that struggle, real sexual tension arises between Gellar and David Boreanaz.

Several of Angel's past appearances were criticized for serving little purpose, but in this episode Angel's presence adds an edge to the show, diluting some of the "fluffiness" of the characters' usual high school problems. And we're hit with a surprising twist when Angel, while kissing Buffy, reveals himself to be a vampire, albeit a reluctant one. We learn that Angel has less in common with the show's usual bloodsuckers than with such predecessors as

Dark Shadows's Barnabas Collins and *Forever Knight*'s Nick Knight, in terms of fighting his true nature in order to live among humans and apart from the other vampires. Subtextually, this raises the question of whether or not redemption is possible for a creature who was a killing machine for hundreds of years. Thanks to a Gypsy curse, resulting from his destroying a particular family a century earlier, he was destined to have his soul returned to him, allowing him to feel guilt over all the people he had murdered over the past hundred years.

The episode features an excellent, if somewhat predictable, scene in which Darla, the vampire, bites Mrs. Summers and sets it up to appear as if Angel did the biting, and Buffy witnesses this. There is a great cut to the outside of Buffy's house when she angrily kicks Angel right through a window.

There are more unusual plot twists as Darla, well aware of Buffy's reputation as a Vampire Slayer, shows up armed with guns, planning to actually shoot Buffy, who's armed only with a crossbow. The idea of a vampire using guns is

a great innovation that only serves to enhance this particular episode. The conclusion of the battle, in which Angel plunges an arrow into Darla's heart, is a truly powerful moment.

There are some perverse moments taking place in the Underworld, where the Master continues to teach the young Anointed One the nuances of dominating others.

Episode Eight: "I Robot, You Jane"

Original Airdate: 4/28/97
Written by Ashley Gable and Thomas A. Swyden
Directed by Stephen Posey
Guest Starring Robia La Morte (Miss Calendar), Chad Lindberg, Jamison Ryan

PRESS SYNOPSIS As a computer teacher tries to lure book-lover Giles into the world of technology, Willow begins a dangerous online romance.

COMMENTARY (✝✝) The idea of exorcism heads toward the twenty-first century in this bizarre episode that essentially deals with demonic possession of the Internet—certainly not an idea you'll find on too many shows. For fans of *Colossus: The Forbin Project* or *2001: A Space Odyssey*, the tale of an errant computer should be an appealing one.

The episode has a very cool beginning that, despite an obviously limited budget, transports us back in time to 1861 Italy and the very original concept of monks performing a ceremony that traps a demon within the pages of a book. Flash forward to the present and Sunnydale High (of course), and we see a student scanning the text of this particular book into the computer, thus unleashing the demon there. On the surface it sounds like a completely absurd concept, but who cares?

There's something touching about Alyson Hannigan's quiet desperation in wanting to meet someone and finding an online pal, "Malcolm," throwing herself into this "relationship" without having any real idea of what she's getting into.

It's amusing to see the demon manipulating the computer, causing financial discrepancies for the Vatican as well as screwing around with medical records and rewriting term papers ("Nazi Germany was a well-organized society? Who's been messing around with my term paper?" asks one incredulous student).

Dopey point: Buffy comes to Giles with an oddity concerning the computer, and he seems skeptical. Given everything they've already seen, when Buffy says, "Jump!" Giles should ask, "How high?" and vice versa. It's kind of like Dana Scully of *The X-Files* bending over backward to explain things scientifically, when you want to grab her by the shoulders and shout, "HELLO!"

Some cute pop culture references: the demon voice on the computer sounds very much like the Hal 9000 computer from *2001* and even goes so far as to manipulate a student named Dave (as in that film's astronaut Dave Bowman); and at one point Buffy tells Giles her "spider-sense is tingling," which she actually describes as a pop culture reference.

When the demon computer starts making students kill each other, you can't help but wonder if somehow this show has become a live-action version of *Rugrats* because the kids seem to know everything and have all these incredible adventures, while the adults are completely oblivious to everything going on around them.

The episode introduces Robia La Morte in the recurring role of Ms. Calendar, a computer teacher who describes herself as a "Techno-Pagan" (which implies that she is some sort of modern witch, albeit a good one). She's very attractive and butts heads with Giles, who is more married to the idea of information coming from books rather than from the Internet.

Things get kind of goofy as the demon's consciousness is expanded from the Web into a funky-looking robot that seems like something out of *Power Rangers.* Nonetheless, the concept works fairly well.

The show's conclusion is just plain silly: an online exorcism is performed by Giles and Ms. Calendar, who remove the demon from the Internet and lock it firmly into the body of the robot. At that point, the robot short-circuits when it tries to punch Buffy but ends up punching, instead, a power grid and electrocutes itself. The storyline doesn't really work, and the logic of the demon therefore being lost to the cosmos as a result doesn't pay off.

Episode Nine: "The Puppet Show"

Original Airdate: 5/5/97
Written by Dean Batali and Rob Des Hotel
Directed by Ellen S. Pressman
Guest Starring Kristine Sutherland, Richard Werner, Burke Roberts, Armin Shimerman

PRESS SYNOPSIS Giles is the reluctant coordinator of a school talent show featuring a ventriloquist whose dummy seems to have a mind of its own.

COMMENTARY (✝✝½) Right at the outset, this episode has a lot going against it, not only because the notion of a living wooden dummy is so old hat, but because it is so incredibly difficult to pull the idea off in a realistic fashion. In fact, the only examples that come to mind that worked at all were an episode of Rod Serling's *The*

Twilight Zone, which was more of a psychological exploration; the original *Child's Play* (which had the benefit of a multimillion dollar budget); and the classic TV movie *Trilogy of Terror,* in which one story portrayed Karen Black terrorized by an African tribal doll that came to life.

Another problem with the episode is the way it's set up: it telegraphs that the dummy is alive so far in advance that the audience spends almost half the show being ahead of the characters, which is not very conducive to holding a viewer's interest.

The cool factor goes up a bit when Giles comes to the conclusion that the dummy, named Sid, is seeking a human heart and brain to remain alive, but then we learn that Sid is actually the *victim* in this situation; that he is actually cursed and desperately wants to destroy the true demon—not so that he can stay a living entity but so that he can at last die and attain peace. In the last 15 minutes of the show, "Sid" goes a long way in making the whole situation fairly believable, although watching him stab another student

who is actually the demon still looks pretty phony.

Armin Shimerman (Pascal from *Beauty and the Beast* and Quark from *Star Trek: Deep Space Nine*) joins the show in the recurring role of Principal Snyder, who's supposed to be much sterner than his predecessor. It remains to be seen where this character will ultimately go, but Snyder is designed to be deadly serious about everything and completely opposed to Flutie's touchy-feely approach ("Which got him eaten," he notes). The problem is that he goes so far in the opposite direction that he runs almost as great a risk of being a caricature of a different kind.

One humorous bit: when a student is killed and his heart seems to have been removed by a common kitchen knife, Buffy, Xander, and Willow seemed incredulous that the murderer could actually be human rather than an offspring of the Hellmouth.

Episode Ten: "Nightmares"

Original Airdate: 5/12/97
Story by Joss Whedon

Teleplay by David Greenwalt
Directed by Bruce Seth Green
*Guest Starring Mark Metcalf, Kristine Suther-
land, Jeremy Foley, Andrew J. Ferchland*

PRESS SYNOPSIS A young boy's accident leaves him comatose, and his unsettled spirit wreaks havoc on Sunnydale.

COMMENTARY (✝✝½) Nightmares brought to reality are certainly nothing new in the realm of science fiction or horror, as this is a theme that has been explored many times, in numerous episodes of *Star Trek: The Next Generation*, the *Nightmare on Elm Street* film series, and elsewhere. This episode of *Buffy*, however, was probably even more inspired by the early seventies horror film *Patrick*. In that movie, a young man has an accident and falls into a coma, but his subconscious mind psychically lashes out at the world around him.

In "Nightmares," young Billy Palmer has been beaten into a coma, and his astral presence is felt all over Sunnydale High, usually appearing be- fore people's nightmares start to come true. One student, plagued with guilt over the death of his spider collection, has repeated nightmares of opening a textbook and unleashing tarantulas all over the classroom, which comes to life (a very well-staged scene that is a true *X-Files* moment—and that's a compliment). Another student, Laura, goes down to the school's basement to sneak a smoke when she's confronted by the "ugly man," a large, lumbering, monster-like being that beats her until she has to be hospitalized. A tough guy in the midst of displaying testosterone to his cronies suddenly meets up with his mother, who begins kissing his cheek and calling him "honey;" Xander is suddenly standing in his underwear in front of his classroom; Willow abruptly finds herself on stage, where she is supposed to perform in an opera, and she is completely unable to sing, which results in her being pelted with fruits and vegetables; Cordelia not only has a bad hair and clothes day, but she is horrified to find herself a member of the track team; Xander has another nightmare that turns into reality when he is chased by a clown from his sixth birthday party—only this time the clown is armed with a knife. Ultimately, Xander learns that by confronting his fear, he can make it disappear.

Giles goes through two living nightmares: the first being that he is unable to read, and the second that he is unable to protect Buffy, whom he thinks is killed by the Master in battle, and he blames himself for her demise.

Buffy, naturally, has the most diverse nightmares. On a mortal level, she must take a test that she has no knowledge of and that there is simply no time to complete because the class period is over almost as soon as it begins. Things get worse, when she believes her deepest fear has come true: that she was the cause of her parents' breakup. Indeed, her father shows up at school and decides it's time she know the truth: that the marriage was doomed from the moment she was born and that she has been a major disappointment. Kudos to Gellar for pulling off Buffy's pain and tears so successfully in this scene without resorting to histrionics. Her silent suffering is more powerful than any sobbing could ever be.

Her nightmares as a Slayer are considerably different: she fears that the Master will be able to reach Earth and that she will be completely helpless to defeat him; that he, in turn, will bury her alive; and that she will ultimately be turned into a vampire. Not your average nightmares, to be sure.

By the end, it all centers around Billy Palmer and the efforts of our heroes to revive him, which are made possible when Billy's Kiddy League coach checks up on him, and it's revealed that he blamed Billy for losing the game and beat him up for it. Unfortunately, this revelation and the man's effortless capture are all fairly unexciting. Things wrap up far too easily and that's a pity, because the build-up was pretty suspenseful.

Episode Eleven: "Invisible Girl" (a.k.a. "Out of Mind, Out of Sight")

Original Airdate: 5/19/97
Story by Joss Whedon

Teleplay by Ashley Gable and Thomas A. Swyden
Directed by Reza Badiyi
Guest Starring David Boreanaz, Clea DuVall, Armin Shimerman

PRESS SYNOPSIS An ignored student takes revenge on those who tormented her.

COMMENTARY (✝✝) Although you probably never noticed them, certain individuals among all high school student bodies go unnoticed by everyone around them, from their fellow students to teachers who are somehow oblivious to their presence. "Invisible Girl" starts off with this premise and gives it the usual dark twist that turns a traditional story into an episode of *Buffy*.

The show begins, interestingly enough, as Cordelia's date is changing in the gym locker room, where he is assaulted by a self-propelled baseball bat. It's a well-staged effect, and not a moment you're likely to find on a repeat of *Bewitched* or *I Dream of Jeannie*.

Unfortunately, something of a false note is struck pretty early on. Buffy feels left out because of Cordelia's put-downs, while banter between Xander and Willow about their childhoods just adds fuel to that fire. It seems that after eleven episodes of the show—after we've experienced many adventures "alongside" of Buffy—it should be obvious to everyone, including our Slayer, that Cordelia is a bimbo and she should completely get over herself.

What *does* work in this episode is the initial belief on the part of Buffy, Giles, and the team that they're dealing with a poltergeist of some sort until they finally come to the conclusion that they're dealing with a student who can somehow turn herself invisible. Of course, the revelation is that this invisible girl, Marcie Ross, was someone who had been so ignored that she literally faded away. Blaming Cordelia for much of the unhappiness in her life, Marcie sets out to get revenge.

Look for a well-executed third act in which Marcie captures both Cordelia and Buffy, planning to perform a bit of surgery on Cordelia's often commented upon face. We know Buffy is going to ultimately save the day, but things actually do get suspenseful on the way there. Kudos to director Reza Badiyi for getting so much mileage out of something that, on paper, could have been extremely lame.

A nice moment: Angel returns, meets with Giles, and the two of them discuss the Master, with Angel saying that he can get his hands on a missing book of prophecies concerning the Slayer. It's a brief scene, having more to do with the season finale than with the episode at hand, but it does provide a poignant opportunity to explore the tragedy of Angel's existence, when the vampire states that he wishes he could even see his own reflection in a mirror. There's also, finally, an attempt to explore Cordelia's character, providing some insight into the insecurities that fuel her bitchy persona. Nice touch.

A dopey moment: Several guys in suits are hanging around the school throughout the episode, and it takes forever for someone to comment on their presence. It's no big surprise that they turn out to be government agents, although their leaving the school grounds with Marcie is. The

episode's coda, a bit too quickly staged to be really effective, has invisible Marcie being brought to a classroom of other invisible students, all of whom are being trained by the government as special agents.

All said and done, an average episode.

Episode Twelve: "Prophesy Girl"

Original Airdate: 6/2/97
Written and Directed by Joss Whedon
Guest Starring Mark Metcalf, David Boreanaz, Kristine Sutherland, Robia La Morte, Andrew J. Ferchland

PRESS SYNOPSIS Giles's books predict that Buffy is about to face the Master in a battle to the death—hers.

COMMENTARY (✝✝✝) Series creator/executive producer Joss Whedon serves as writer and director of this episode, demonstrating why they pay him the big bucks. "Prophesy Girl" is a quintessential episode of *Buffy the Vampire Slayer*, with a tense through-line, riveting moments of characterization, well-staged fight scenes, and plenty of humor created from the situation rather than from dopey one-liners.

As was set up in the previous episode, Angel brings Giles a missing book of Slayer prophecies, in which it is revealed that Buffy will go up in battle against the Master and die as a result. Initially, there's no reason to believe the threat is very real—you know, there's the usual television argument that you can't do serious damage to your lead or else your show is over. Yet in only a short matter of time, your confidence is shaken. While Giles's stuttering around Buffy or heated, whispered conversations with Angel belie the nature of what's supposed to happen according to the prophesy, it is Sarah Michelle Gellar's performance as Buffy that makes everything take root. She overhears Giles and Angel talking, and her resulting anger and fear are tangible things. It's easily the actress's best performance as Buffy, highlighted by her pleading statement, "I'm sixteen years old. . . . I don't want to die."

The high point of the episode is the moment the Anointed One (or Damien, as I prefer to call him) leads Buffy to the Underworld and the lair of the Master. Unfortunately, Buffy isn't able to offer much of a threat, and when the Master bites her, informs her that it is her blood that ultimately gives him the strength to leave (in other words, had she not come to him, he never would have gotten out of there), and then drops her seemingly lifeless body into a pool of water, it's a pretty heavy and shocking moment. For an instant, you wonder whether or not someone will show up to rescue her. Just as you're starting to give up hope, Angel and Xander arrive on the scene. A few CPR moves later and Buffy revives, feeling stronger and more confident than she ever has, and she goes out after the Master, dispatching him in a well-edited battle.

If there's a complaint to be lodged regarding this whole act, it's that we're never really provided with much of an explanation as to exactly *why* Buffy seems so much stronger after she died (hence emphasizing the validity of the prophesy discussed at the outset) and how she's suddenly able to accomplish all that she does.

Gellar isn't the only person who is allowed to shine in the episode. Xander finally works up the courage to ask Buffy out on a date—practicing his "pitch" on the adoring Willow—and ultimately is rejected by Buffy because she doesn't want to ruin their friendship. Brendon does a great job showcasing the character's initial nervousness and then his rejection, really touching your heart. Even more, Alyson Hannigan's silent suffering as Willow can't help but move you. Mark Metcalf gives

his best performance as the Master, delivering his usual one-liners but proving particularly effective in the game of cat-and-mouse he initiates with Buffy once she comes to his realm.

This season finale brought the series to an interesting place. Because the series had not aired during the production of its first 12 episodes, no one was sure how the audience was going to respond to it. If *Buffy* had tanked in the ratings and was canceled after the initial 12 shows, there was, thanks to Whedon's careful planning, an ending of sorts to the series. Thankfully, it wasn't necessary.

SEASON TWO
Cast

Sarah Michelle Geller
(Buffy Summers)

Nicholas Brendon
(Xander Harris)

Alyson Hannigan
(Willow Rosenberg)

Charisma Carpenter
(Cordelia Chase)

David Boreanaz
(Angel)

Anthony Stewart Head
(Rupert Giles)

Crew

EXECUTIVE PRODUCERS
Joss Whedon, Sandy Gallin, Gail
Berman, Fran Rubel Kuzui, Kaz Kuzui

CO-EXECUTIVE PRODUCER
David Greenwalt

CO-PRODUCERS
David Solomon, Gary Law

CONSULTING PRODUCER
Howard Gordon

EXECUTIVE STORY EDITORS
Rob Des Hotel and Dean Batali

STORY EDITOR
Marti Noxon

SCORE BY
Christopher Beck, Adam Fields, Shawn
K. Clement, Sean Murray

THEME BY
Nerf Herder

DIRECTORS OF PHOTOGRAPHY
Michael Gershman,
Kenneth D. Zunder

PRODUCTION DESIGNER
Carey Meyer

Episode Thirteen: "When She Was Bad"

Original Airdate: 9/15/97
Written and Directed by Joss Whedon
Guest Starring Robia La Morte (Ms. Calendar), Andrew J. Ferchland (The Annointed One), Dean Butler (Hank Summers), Brent Jennings (Absalom), Armin Shimerman (Principal Snyder), Tamara Braun (Tara)

PRESS SYNOPSIS Buffy must finally put the Master to rest for all time. Giles is the link to the Master's return from the dead, only no one realizes his importance until Buffy goes out on a wild goose chase.

COMMENTARY (✝✝✝) Dying and being brought back to life are liable to bring up a variety of reactions in someone, but in Buffy's case they seem to have brought on a *major* case of PMS. When we meet her again after the summer vacation (read: "hiatus"), she is angry, defiant, and distant from all her friends. Either it was her battle with the Master at the end of season one, or Sarah Michelle Gellar was really pissed off because she was so tired, having segued from season one of *Buffy* to *I Know What You Did Last Summer* and *Scream 2*, which she had to shoot on weekends while shooting *Buffy* Monday through Friday. This was one exhausted lady.

One of the strongest attributes of the series is that there are consequences for actions taken in each episode. Although we're never really told why Buffy has gone through such a transformation, given her attitudes at the end of season one, when we're reintroduced to the character she has gone into a dark place that no one—not even Angel—can reach. As a result, the tension between the characters is tangible, particularly when Buffy is manipulating virtually everyone (look for her *very* erotic dance with poor Xander, designed to make Angel jealous), even to the point that she is trying to bait Angel into a fight to the death.

The fight sequences are extremely well-choreographed, with an intensity that many of the previous fights had never achieved: Gellar comes across more like Rambo than Buffy. In all likelihood, Gellar, in a summer when she was forced to play a victim in movies, probably enjoyed the opportunity to kick some ass instead. The episode has a great closing moment, when a tearful Buffy completely obliterates the skeletal remains of the Master (whom the vampires were trying to resurrect) while cathartically casting off her personal mental demons at the same time.

Two interesting moments: Xander and Willow come damn close to kissing in the show's teaser, until Buffy suddenly shows up, scuttling what could have been an interesting relationship. That near-kiss, inspired by some ice cream that got on Willow's nose, is pretty much dropped, except for a moment when she smears cream on herself and points it out to Xander, who dismisses it with, "You've got something on your nose." Your heart really does break for this girl. There's also the sequence in which Cordelia—finally starting to play a more significant role in the show—tries to warn Buffy to chill out or she'll lose her "loser" friends. Again, a nice bit of character growth, which is so important in dramatic episodic television.

Episode Fourteen: "Some Assembly Required"

Original Airdate: 9/22/97
Written by Ty King
Directed by Bruce Seth Green
Guest Starring Robia La Morte (Ms. Calendar), Angelo Spizzirri (Chris), Michael
Bacall (Eric), Ingo Neuhaus (Daryl), Melanie MacQueen (Mrs. Epps), Amanda Wilmhurst (Cheerleader)

PRESS SYNOPSIS   Beautiful teenage girls turn up in the morgue, but they are missing body parts. A madman is building his dream women piece by piece, and Buffy and Cordelia become his final objects of desire.

COMMENTARY (✝✝½)   While most episodic television, particularly in this genre (except for, perhaps, *Deep Space Nine* and *Babylon 5*) goes out of its way to provide standalone episodes with little continuity, *Buffy* is proving itself to be just the opposite. Yes, the storyline of "Some Assembly Required" is pretty much a standalone show, but the characterizations continue the arc started in the previous episode. This is particularly true in terms of the aftermath of Buffy's somewhat erotically charged dance with Xander in the season premiere, which hurt Xander's feelings and fulfilled Buffy's purpose of making Angel jealous. While there's no great pleasure in seeing people suffer, it does bring a level of realism to the proceedings. One only wishes that Xander would stop complaining about being alone and open his eyes (as he almost did in "When She Was Bad") and see how much Willow really cares for him.

Cordelia, as vacuous as she is, continues to grow (albeit slowly), accepting what she's seen and playing a more significant role than she has in the past. She moves beyond just being the pretty and popular bitch in school. It's amusing to watch her pursuit of Angel, because she is completely unaware of his true nature.

Anthony Stewart Head gets to shine a bit as Giles embarks on the first stages of a relationship with Ms. Calendar, when the two of them go out on their first date.

One character highlight is Angel's frustration that he can only see Buffy at night, and their walking off hand in hand at the conclusion is a nice moment, making the audience wonder just where this "Beauty and the Beast"–like relationship will ultimately go.

The storyline itself seems like a combination of *Frankenstein*, *Reanimator*, and *Weird Science*, as a couple of science geeks take a stab at resurrection. While we're given a sense of brotherly love (and how far one brother will go to make his sibling happy, yadda, yadda, yadda), this part of the story, amazingly—despite the appropriate pyrotechnics and some effective battles—is the least interesting part of the episode. Admittedly, though, what other show would have cheerleaders being killed so that a perfect corpse could be created?

The bottom line is that we get the greatest amount of pleasure in this episode from watching the expansion of the characterizations.

Episode Fifteen: "School Hard"

Original Airdate: 9/29/97
Written by David Greenwalt
Directed by John Kretchmer
Guest Starring Robia La Morte (Ms. Calendar), Andrew J. Ferchland (The Anointed One), James Marsters (Spike),

In most television shows, there is an episode—usually pretty early in its run—where all of the elements come together creatively and say, in essence, "This is what our show is capable of achieving." On Star Trek: The Next Generation it was "Where No One Has Gone Before" and on The X-Files it was "Ice." For Buffy the Vampire Slayer, it is undoubtedly "Angel."

Alexandra Johnes (Sheila), Juliet Landau (Drusilla), Armin Shimerman (Principal Snyder), Keith Mackechnie (Parent), Alan Abelew (Brian Kirch), Joanie Pleasant (Helpless Girl)

PRESS SYNOPSIS
This episode contains the introduction of Spike and Drusilla, the vampires even the Anointed One doesn't cross. Buffy must face the only vampire known to kill two Slayers, while keeping her secret from her mom.

COMMENTARY
(✝✝½) The *Buffy* storyline takes a new direction in its ongoing vampire arc with the introduction of James Marsters (Spike) and the whacked-out Drusilla (Juliet Landau), who Joss Whedon has referred to as Sid and Nancy, and with good reason.

Spike is the ultimate punk rocker: a guy with an attitude who walks into a room and takes it over. Unlike so many others who merely talk the talk, he actually has the power to back up his words and attitude. Drusilla's a little harder to figure out, coming across more like someone who has indulged in one too many drugs and is scrambling to recover whatever brain cells she can. Nonetheless, the two of them play off each other nicely, and Spike brings with him a welcome bit of in-your-face humor. However, what's strange about Spike's presence on the show is that when he's in the Underworld among the other vampires, he is menacing and definitely in charge. When he's on the surface, threatening Buffy and her team, somehow his strength seems diminished, his threat not quite as real as it is underground. A difficult conundrum to figure out.

The school plot of the episode has Buffy and a trouble-making student named Sheila put in charge of Parent–Teacher Night by the increasingly annoying Principal Snyder, who utters some of the dopiest lines ever offered about students and does so with such seriousness that you can't wait for vampires to sink their fangs into his neck (unfortunately, this never happens).

Watching Buffy balance her responsibility with her ongoing battles with the undead doesn't really work here. The vampires come a callin' to kill her that evening, but Snyder and all the parents think they're just a rowdy bunch of punks causing trouble. Indeed, that's the category that Buffy is again put into, with everyone bringing up that she has a troubled past (been there, done that—move along, people) and burned down her old school's gymnasium. Even her mother gets into the act, telling her to get "into the car" when Snyder provides information about Buffy's academic performance. Mom has a change of heart, however, when she sees Buffy in action, saving everyone she can. Not realizing that the people that her daughter is battling are vampires, she actually expresses her pride in the fact that Buffy would risk her own life to help her friends. Mother and daughter reach a new state of trust and respect for each other—which Buffy predicts will last about a week and a half.

A few effective moments occur between Spike and Angel, where we learn a bit more about Angel's past. There's also a nice pop culture reference, which nonetheless seems very real, when Spike, distraught that Angel has changed his ways, shouts, "You were my sire, man; my Yoda."

Great scene: Spike, saying they need to have a little fun in the Underworld, takes the Anointed One, locks him in a cage, and unceremoniously raises him into sunlight, where he's destroyed. Hysterically funny, in the way that the staff simply writes out a character that they probably didn't know what the hell to do with.

The episode's a little sloppier than is the norm for *Buffy*. For instance, we see Sheila snatched by vampires and watch as she's bitten; this makes the audience fully aware that when she shows up for Parent–Teacher Night there will come a point when she'll reveal herself to be a vampire. This was badly telegraphed and disappointing.

Probably the biggest disappointment about the episode is the coda in which Snyder and a cop are talking about the situation, essentially admitting that they're well aware that vampires are in Sunnydale, thus implying an *X-Files*–like government conspiracy. I hope this idea will be dropped, because it seriously mars a show that has shown a tremendous amount of originality.

Episode Sixteen: "Inca Mummy Girl"

Original Airdate: 10/6/97
Written by Matt Kiene and Joe Reinkemeyer
Directed by Ellen Pressman
Guest Starring Kristine Sutherland (Joyce Summers), Ara Celi (Mummy/Ampata), Seth Green (Oz), Jason Hall (Devon), Henrik Rosvall (Sven), Joey Crawford (Rodney), Danny Strong (Jonathan), Kristen Winnicki (Gwen), Gil Birmingham (Peru Man), Samuel Jacobs (Peruvian Boy/Real Ampata)

PRESS SYNOPSIS Xander falls for a beautiful Peruvian exchange student staying with Buffy, only to face death when the object of his love is revealed to be an ancient mummy who needs to kill to stay alive.

COMMENTARY (✝✝) There are some guys who simply don't have luck with women, and our friend Xander is definitely one of them. As if his experience with the giant praying mantis ("Teacher's Pet," events of which are mentioned in this episode) wasn't enough, here he has to cope with Mummy-Girl Ampata, who must mummify people to gain their life force in order to stay alive.

Although the pacing of the episode is off in comparison to other shows, there are nonetheless some interesting character moments. Gellar and Anthony Stewart Head continue their never-boring repartee in Buffy's never-ending attempt to balance her life as a teenager with her destiny as a Slayer. Actually, despite a few scenes each, the real focus of the episode seems to be on Xander, who once again falls in love with the wrong woman—in this case, Ampata. As usual, Nicholas Brendon comes across very real despite his occasional goofiness, and when things go wrong, as we know they inevitably will, his pain becomes our own. Same for Alyson Hannigan, who manages to

not seem tiresome in her own suffering over watching Xander fall for yet another girl; later, she gives in to infectious glee when Ampata turns out to be a mummy.

The nice surprise here is the character of Ampata, who manages to remain sympathetic despite having to mummify people in order to live. She was killed at a young age and was never given the opportunity to live a full life, so there's some pathos in her existence and you're left with the feeling that you wish someone had come up with a way to save her rather than allow her to crumble to dust at the end (which happens to mummies much more often than you might think). Look for some cool effects in the climactic scenes, which also happen to be pretty suspenseful as Xander nearly sacrifices himself so that Willow can live; luckily, he's saved by Buffy, who's returning the favor from "Prophesy Girl."

It's also interesting to watch the successful tapdancing of the writing staff, as they continue to come up with different ways of bringing supernatural threats to Sunnydale. In this particular case, a "Cultural Exchange Week" is the impetus for ultimately getting Ampata to Sunnydale.

There's some hope for Willow in this episode: she finds herself the object of affection of a drummer named Oz (Seth Green), who's looking for a woman with brains (Willow) rather than someone with looks and not much else going for her (Cordelia). Although not much happens between them in this particular episode, we're definitely left with the feeling that something might happen in the future.

Episode Seventeen: "Reptile Boy"

Original Airdate: 10/13/97
Written and Directed by David Greenwalt
Guest Starring Greg Vaughn (Richard), Todd Babcock (Tom), Jordana Spiro (Callie)

PRESS SYNOPSIS   A party at a very prestigious, wealthy frat house turns ugly for Buffy and Cordelia when they realize they're going to be sacrificed to the fraternity's Savior, Reptile Boy.

COMMENTARY (✝✝)   The annals of the horrors of high school life continue, as Buffy and Cordelia venture into the previously unexplored world of college fraternities. While Cordelia is excited to be doing so, Buffy joins her reluctantly.

Naturally, because nothing relatively normal can happen on *Buffy the Vampire Slayer* (or the show would be called *Beverly Hills 90210*), it isn't long before what seem to be drunk, drug-the-girl-so-I-can-sleep-with-her college morons, turn out to be something much darker. The idea that this fraternity actually worships a snake-like demon is a hoot and is pulled off pretty effectively, avoiding what could have been a traditional serial killer/slasher storyline.

This episode, despite a few suspenseful action moments, is more concerned with exploring the characters than anything else. First, we get to scrutinize the developing relationship between Buffy and Angel (in scenes that usually end with one of them stalking off angrily), with Angel seemingly putting the brakes on things because of the difference in their ages (what's two hundred years between friends?) and the fact that passion seems to bring out his darker impulses. In fact, going their separate ways turns out to be the impetus for Buffy to visit the frat house with Cordelia in the first place. There is an interesting wrap-up to this when Angel (implying a bit of Vincent, the lion-man from TV's *Beauty and the Beast*) fangs out when he learns that Buffy's in danger (though, ironically, she handles herself just fine without his help). An "aw, shucks" moment occurs at the end of the episode when the couple decides to go out for a cup of coffee, giving the impression that maybe they will give their relationship a shot after all.

Cordelia is the real surprise here. Thankfully, the writers really seem to be making an effort to move the character beyond the apparent limitations set up in the first season. Besides partaking in more slaying activities, she is allowed to be seen completely out of her element and floundering. While she seems in control of her life in high school (although we've heard about her earlier insecurities), she is completely out of her league on a college campus—even without the frat boys actually being a reptilian cult.

Our man Xander is also given the opportunity to strut his stuff, being the hero and attempting to rescue Buffy and Cordelia. In fact, the feeling is that the seeds are actually being planted for *something* to happen between Xander and Cordelia, which would be interesting considering the number of times Xander has asked her out and been rebuked or just put down in general. That they can grow closer at all (even if it's just on Xander's part, for the moment), just shows that the writing staff is devoting an incredible amount of energy to beefing up the characters surrounding Buffy.

Episode Eighteen: "Halloween"

Original Airdate: 10/27/97
Written by Carl Ellsworth
Directed by Bruce Seth Green
Guest Starring Seth Green (Oz), James
*   Marsters (Spike), Robin Sachs (Ethan),*

Juliet Landau (Drusilla), Armin Shimerman (Principal Snyder)

PRESS SYNOPSIS Although Halloween is traditionally a quiet night for Slayers, this turns out not to be the case when someone from Giles's past has the power to transform Buffy, Willow, Xander, and all the children they're chaperoning into the characters depicted by their Halloween costumes. This could prove to be deadly for Buffy when she loses her slaying ability because her choice of costume is an eighteenth-century noblewoman whom Buffy thinks was romantically involved with Angel.

COMMENTARY (✝✝✝) One can only imagine the writers of this series sitting around the office trying to come up with new and innovative ways to tell the stories that make up *Buffy the Vampire Slayer*. This concept—the idea that magic can make people turn into the characters they've dressed as for Halloween—seems fairly original. The means of getting there is a bit contrived (Principal Sny-

der forcing the gang to take kids out trick-or-treating, with the express instruction that they be in costume), but the end result is worth it. Plus, it provides the opportunity for some humorous moments as Xander explains to the kids the secrets of successful trick-or-treating.

The character of Ethan (Robin Sachs) represents a truly evil human being (gifted with malevolent powers) and where he shines is in his ability to bring out Giles's darker nature (seeing him pummel the man for information on how to reverse the spell is pretty shocking stuff). We're also left wondering just what kind of background the seemingly shy librarian comes from, what sordid secrets he carries with him. Unfortunately, all the audience can do is hope that Ethan—who, unlike most of the villains of the show, gets away at the end—will return.

The true highlight of the show is watching Willow do so much to save the day when she acquires the ghost-like powers that go with her costume; Xander's personality turning darker as a soldier (something Nicholas Brendon does so well, as was previously explored in "The Pack"); and Buffy providing a bit of humor as an English noblewoman with a penchant for fainting.

Probably one of the most interesting aspects of the episode is Spike's having a vampire videotape Buffy in battle with another vampire, in the hopes that he can study her in action and learn her weaknesses. A truly innovative twist to a vampire story and so far removed from the setting of Bram Stoker's *Dracula* and the vast majority of vampire films.

Speaking of Spike, his scenes with Drusilla continue to be simultaneously weird and touching—weird in the sense that Drusilla seems so unaware of the world around her yet psychically very much in tune with everything, and touching in that Spike seems so gentle, patient, and different with her than with anyone else. It's reassuring that upon coming up with a replacement for the Master, Joss Whedon and the writing staff didn't elect to clone the same kind of character, choosing instead to go in quite a different direction.

Episode Nineteen: "Lie to Me"

Original Airdate: 11/3/97
Written and Directed by Joss Whedon
Guest Starring Robia La Morte (Ms. Calendar), James Marsters (Spike), Jason Behr (Bill "Ford" Fordham), Jarrad Paul (Marvin "Diego"), Juliet Landau (Drusilla), Will Rothhaar (James), Julia Lee (Chanterella)

PRESS SYNOPSIS A boyfriend from Buffy's past attempts to deliver her to Spike in exchange for the immortality of being a vampire.

COMMENTARY (✝✝✝) Being stricken with a life-threatening illness is liable to make even the most noble person consider a darker path. It's that motivation on the part of Bill "Ford" Fordham (Jason Behr) that drives this episode of *Buffy*. In the course of the show, the guy does a lot of sick things and tries to manipulate everyone around him, believing that his six-month life expectancy entitles him to do whatever is necessary to survive. His solution is pretty inventive: to serve

Buffy and a group of vampire cultists up for dinner, with all of the intended believing that they'll gain immortality and oblivious to the fact that in all likelihood they'll be used for nothing more than fodder.

Ford's interaction with Spike and his never-ending quest to secretly hand Buffy over to him is interesting, but the meat and potatoes of the episode come from Buffy's frustrations over her relationship with Angel and what we learn about his background as well as his past relationship with Drusilla. As a result, Drusilla, who had come across as little more than a psychic, vicious vampiric loon in the past, actually manages to be more sympathetic.

Apparently, it was Angel who turned Drusilla into a vampire in the first place, but it was not a simple kill. Angel, in full demonic mindset, decided that it would be fun to psychologically torture her by slowly killing her friends and family and following her everywhere she went. Looking for solace, she turned to the church and attempted to become one with God by entering a convent, but at the last pos-

sible moment Angel turned her into a vampire.

It's an extremely powerful revelation, and its impact is immediately felt by Buffy, as evidenced by Sarah Michelle Gellar's wonderful performance in this scene. What it serves to do, once again, is show us the depths from which Angel has come and how much he has accomplished in terms of keeping his darker nature at bay. It's also a gutsy move on the part of the writers to give a simpatico character such a sordid past. In a sense, though, he's more heroic for overcoming it.

The tag of the episode is spectacular. Buffy, shouldering the emotional weight of the story, is looking for some reassurance from Giles that the world isn't as bad a place as it seems. Giles does his best to comply, facetiously telling her what she wants to hear, but is interrupted when Ford, now a vampire, rises from his grave and Buffy unceremoniously stakes and kills him. Without missing a beat, she says to Giles, "Liar." An inspired moment.

A dopey point: There's no real explanation for how Ford knows Buffy is a Slayer, which he clearly does from the moment he shows up. He did know her in the past at her other school, so it's possible that's where he discovered it, but some sort of statement would have been nice. Still, a minor quibble in a terrific episode.

Episode Twenty: "The Dark Age"

Original Airdate: 11/10/97
Written by Dean Batali and Rob Des Hotel
Directed by Bruce Seth Green
Guest Starring Robia La Morte (Ms. Calendar), Robin Sachs (Ethan), Stuart McLean (Philip Henry), Wendy Way (Dierdre), Michael Earl Reid (Custodian), Daniel Henry Murray (Creep Cult Guy), Carlease Burke (Detective Winslow), Tony Sears (Morgue Attendant), John Bellucci (Man)

PRESS SYNOPSIS   As a youth, Giles rebelled against his destiny of being a Watcher. Unfortunately, that decision returns to haunt him now when friends who know his secret begin turning up dead.

COMMENTARY (✝✝✝)   *Buffy the Vampire Slayer* is rapidly becoming the ultimate book of revelations, as the writers are continually adding real depth to the various characters, painting in backgrounds that aren't necessarily flattering but that have ultimately served to make these people who they are.

In this episode, Giles is the subject/victim at hand. We're given much greater insight into his determination to train Buffy properly, and we come to understand why the moments she doesn't take things seriously really get to him. He's not just being the stereotypical "uptight Brit," he's speaking from past experience. We learn that when he was younger, he rebelled against his destiny of being a Watcher by joining up with several others to travel down a darker road, even going so far as trying to make contact with a demon. It's taken some time, but the demon is finally showing up, dispatching the people who summoned it—despite the fact that in the intervening years Giles came to grips with his destiny.

Anthony Stewart Head is outstanding in this episode, giving us a take on the character that we haven't really seen before—he's disorganized, secretive, distraught, and (to borrow a phrase from *Ally McBeal*), snappish. We also get to see the depths of his concern for Ms. Calendar, once it becomes apparent that she's possessed by the demon, and the guilt he feels for having unleashed this creature in the first place. The return of Ethan (Robin Sachs) not only serves to enhance the continuity within the series but continues to add—not to belabor the point—depth to the Giles character.

It's also reassuring to see the impact of various events on the characters who live out the adventures. Whereas most shows would have probably ended with Giles and Ms. Calendar walking off arm in arm now that the danger has passed, *Buffy* chooses, instead, to have Ms. Calendar react not only to what she's been through in this episode (being possessed by a demon and all) but to what she has learned about Giles as well. Her needing a bit of distance for a while is a perfectly rea-

sonable request and rings true for the character.

There is a great ending sequence in which the demon enters Angel's body and is taken on—and ultimately defeated—by the demon that's already in residence there. A really unique moment.

Episode Twenty-One: "What's My Line?, Part 1"

Original Airdate: 11/17/97
Written by Marti Noxon and Howard Gordon
Directed by David Solomon
Guest Starring Seth Green (Oz), James Marsters (Spike), Eric Saiet (Dalton), Kelly Connell (Norman Pfister), Bianca Lawson (Kendra), Saverio Guerra (Willy), Juliet Landau (Drusilla), Armin Shimerman (Principal Snyder), Michael Rothhaar (Suitman), P. B. Hutton (Mrs. Kalish)

PRESS SYNOPSIS While Spike works on restoring Drusilla to full health, he unleashes vampire bounty hunters in an effort to be rid of Buffy once and for all. In the meantime,

Buffy meets up with another Slayer named Kendra.

COMMENTARY (✝✝✝½) The bottom line is that this series excels best when it's dealing with vampires, in much the same way that *The X-Files* is able to best explore the characters of Mulder and Scully in the so-called mythology episodes.

Spike, in an attempt to help Drusilla, begins to conduct an ancient ceremony but is so fearful that Buffy will interfere that he enlists the aid of vampire bounty hunters, known as the Order of Turaca. These dudes are unlike any vampires we've seen before, hellbent on carrying out their mission no matter what. They're an unexpected breed, but not quite as unexpected as the arrival of Kendra the Vampire Slayer, who was presumably given her destiny at the moment that Buffy stopped breathing in the season one finale, "Prophesy Girl." She is determined to not only kill Angel but his girlfriend as well.

The episode ends with a hell of a cliffhanger: just about everyone is in some kind of danger, an unusual situation. Usually at the end of the first part of a two-parter, one or two characters are threatened. In this case, it's been expanded to just about all of them.

Great moment: Angel engages in battle and is slightly wounded as a result. Buffy tries to offer some sympathy and he's actually shy to have her touch him when he's in full vampire facial regalia. It's a tremendously tender scene, bearing more than a little similarity to many moments between lion-man Vincent and his human love, Catherine, on *Beauty and the Beast*. Given that former *B&B* producer Howard Gordon serves as a consultant on *Buffy* and co-wrote this episode, it's not really a complete surprise.

Interesting character bits: Xander and Cordelia are rapidly becoming the team within the team, spending a lot of time doing the grunt work while simultaneously getting themselves into a hell of a lot of danger. At the same time, they're always in character, with Xander spouting his never-ending stream of one-liners and Cordelia still susceptible to the trappings of her more vacuous existence before joining the Slayer party. This point is evidenced by her willingness to let a cosmetics salesman into the house, oblivious to the fact that he's actually one of the Bounty Hunters. Given what she knows these days, it's surprising she would be this stupid, but that's Cordelia.

We also get to see Willow become positively Watcher-like in her efforts to research on the Internet the situation that they find themselves involved in. What Giles is able to accomplish via the numerous tomes making up the library, Willow is doing via the computer. To some degree, her personality seems to be evolving into a much wiser one than that of the young girl we met at the beginning of the series. On a personal level, she gets to interact with Oz (Seth Green) a bit, and there are implications that something may happen between them in the future.

From every department, the episode is a winner. Kudos to all.

Episode Twenty-Two: "What's My Line?, Part 2"

Original Airdate: 11/24/97
Written by Marti Noxon
Directed by David Semel
Guest Starring Seth Green (Oz), Saverio Guerra (Willy), Bianca Lawson (Kendra), James Marsters (Spike), Juliet Landau (Drusilla), Kelly Connell (Norman Pfister), Spice Williams (Patrice)

PRESS SYNOPSIS Buffy must deal with her insecurities about the existence of another Slayer, while at the same time she must rescue the captured Angel from the torturing hands of Drusilla.

COMMENTARY (✝✝✝½) Oftentimes when *Star Trek: The Next Generation* would do a two-part episode, the inevitable outcome would be that part one was a tremendous build-up, while part two was usually something of a let-down. Thankfully, *Buffy the Vampire Slayer* seems immune to a similar type of formula. "What's My Line?, Part 2" is every bit as exciting as its predecessor, offering even more in the way of characterization.

The vampire battles are extremely well choreographed, and the combination of Spike and Drusilla is proving itself to be more inventive as time goes on. Interestingly, as part of the ceremony to make her normal (relatively speaking, of course), Drusilla captures Angel, as he was the one who turned her into a vampire in the first place. Previously, we had heard about the hell that Angel had put her through when he had no conscience and took great pleasure out of psychological torture. Well, it may have taken her a couple of centuries, but in this episode Drusilla gets retribution.

Incredible power and pathos are created in the sequences in which Angel is trapped in a cage, as Drusilla torments him with Holy Water that burns his skin, all the while awaiting the sunrise that will ultimately destroy him. The scene—very character-based, despite the horrors of what's going on— is a true highlight of the episode and the series as a whole. Credit really has

to go to David Boreanaz and Juliet Landau for pulling this off so well.

Within the action, romance seems to be blossoming for several of the regulars. Amazingly, Xander and Cordelia share not one but two kisses, which are pretty damn passionate. Your heart would break for Willow, except for the fact that Oz has saved her life, moving them ever closer to starting a relationship with each other. Guest star Seth Green manages to be both charming and intense, making Oz a character that you want to watch to see where he goes.

Guest star Bianca Lawson (despite a phony-sounding Jamaican accent) brings an edge to her character of Kendra, offering us a Slayer who is quite different from Buffy. She also nicely conveys the tragic aspects of Kendra in that she has literally spent her whole life training to be a Slayer, helped in no small part by her parents who handed her over to her Watcher years earlier. Now she can barely remember her mother and father and has had nothing else in her life. It's probably enough to give Buffy pause, though at the same time Kendra also triggers a variety of interesting reactions. Case in point: Gellar's nice handling of Buffy's insecurities, wondering whether she's good enough with Kendra on the job. It's not the kind of situation you expect to find her in, but somehow it's appropriate, given the episode's high school backdrop of Career Week (which gives rise to Buffy's question of how she'll earn a living if her "career" is that of a Vampire Slayer). Even if we never see Kendra again, there's something cool about Buffy not being alone any longer, knowing that there is another Slayer out there somewhere.

Episode Twenty-Three: "Ted"

Original Airdate: 12/8/97
Written by David Greenwalt and Joss Whedon
Directed by Bruce Seth Green
Guest Starring John Ritter (Ted Buchanan),
    Kristine Sutherland (Joyce Summers), Robia La Morte (Ms. Calendar), Ken Thorley

(Neal), James G. MacDonald (Detective Stein), Jeff Pruitt (Vampire #1), Jeff Langton (Vampire #2)

PRESS SYNOPSIS   The whole gang falls for Buffy's mom's (Kristine Sutherland) new boyfriend, Ted (guest star John Ritter, "Three's Company")—everyone, that is, except Buffy, who suspects there may be more to him than meets the eye. Meanwhile, Giles tries to repair his relationship with Ms. Calendar (Robia La Morte) after her near-death experience with a demon, and, still reluctant to let anyone know about their romantic involvement, Xander and Cordelia continue to hide their rendezvous from their friends.

COMMENTARY (✝✝)   Well, they can't all be winners. "Ted" is an off episode of *Buffy,* and a good portion of its time is devoted to Mrs. Summers's relationship with Ted (guest star John Ritter), with numerous incidents that supposedly show everyone what a terrific guy he is. Buffy, of course, is the one who suspects that there's something odd about him, and on the occasions that he actually threatens her you know that her feelings are absolutely right.

Initially, Ted comes across as just another abusive jerk/potential stepfather that you could find in any number of television shows. The ultimate revelation that he is a murderous robot who marries women and then kills them at least provides the show with a much-needed *Buffy* twist, but there simply isn't that much to the episode. Ritter, a fine actor, handles his scenes well, but he is not able to make this story come truly alive.

What does work, however, are the relationships, particularly Xander and Cordelia, who find themselves attracted to each other even though they can't really stand each other (and it's amusing to watch them try to hide their feelings from their friends). Then there's the situation between Giles and Ms. Calendar. She's still recovering from the experience of being possessed by a demon, and he is trying way too hard to see that she's alright, which is turning her off. Suffice it to say, in the end they start to work out their problems. A middling episode.

Episode Twenty-Four: "Bad Eggs"

Original Airdate: 1/12/98
Written by Marti Noxon
Directed by David Greenwalt
Guest Starring Kristine Sutherland (Joyce Summers), Jeremy Ratchford (Lyle Gorch), James Parks (Tector Gorch), Rick Zieff (Mr. Whitmore), Danny Strong (Jonathan)

PRESS SYNOPSIS Buffy and the gang are introduced to parenting through a school assignment that takes a very rotten turn. Meanwhile, two Wild West vamps (guest stars Jeremy Ratchford and James Parks) come to town hunting for Buffy. At the same time, romance is in the air when Buffy and Angel continue to rendezvous and Xander and Cordelia keep their liaison in the closet.

COMMENTARY (✝✝) An episode obviously designed to just be mindless fun and perhaps as an antidote to many of the darker episodes that had already made up much of the second season. The plot is a mish-mash of any number of genre films, most notably *Alien* and *Invasion of the Body Snatchers,* and offers very little in terms of continuity with the rest of the series.

The viewer is left with an overall feeling that had this episode aired at another time in *Buffy's* run, it would have been perceived as being a fine show, but with all that has happened during this period, it just doesn't seem to fit in.

Episode Twenty-Five: "Surprise"

Original Airdate: 1/19/98
Written by Marti Noxon
Directed by Michael Lange
Guest Starring Seth Green (Oz), Kristine Sutherland (Joyce Summers), Robia La Morte (Ms. Calendar), Brian Thompson (The Judge), Eric Saiet (Dalton), Vincent Schiavelli (Jenny's Uncle), James Marsters (Spike), Juliet Landau (Drusilla)

PRESS SYNOPSIS The fate of the world is at stake when Spike and Drusilla gather the dismembered body parts of the Judge (guest star Brian Thompson)—a demon with a deadly touch—from the ends of the earth as their ultimate weapon to extinguish the Slayer. Meanwhile, Angel's ability to feel human emotion is in jeopardy when he and Buffy share an intimate moment that threatens to destroy his soul.

COMMENTARY (✝✝✝) The episode opens with a bang via a wonderfully surreal dream, highlighted by Buffy and Angel approaching each other in the Bronze. Drusilla appears, stakes Angel, and he reaches out to Buffy just as he disintegrates, their fingers barely missing each other. Nice stuff.

Revelations, revelations, revelations: We learn that Jenny Calendar (Robia La Morte) actually has a hidden agenda of her own, that she has been sent to watch Buffy and Angel. It seems that she is actually of the lineage of the Gypsy family that Angel tormented a century earlier and that placed the curse of a soul on him. She proves herself to be quite manipulative in this

episode, and it seems surprising that no one catches on to it, as her "suggestions" really aren't that helpful at all.

This time out, Drusilla, on the road to mental recovery, seems to have a few more brain cells functioning than usual and is actually pretty frightening in her evilness. Her plan to resurrect the Judge—whose touch can strip the humanity out of his victims—is a worthy one. For his part, guest star Brian Thompson certainly brings the proper presence with him to this heavily made-up role.

BECAUSE THE SERIES HAD NOT AIRED DURING THE PRODUCTION OF ITS FIRST 12 EPISODES, NO ONE WAS SURE HOW THE AUDIENCE WAS GOING TO RESPOND TO IT. IF BUFFY HAD TANKED IN THE RATINGS AND WAS CANCELLED AFTER THE INITIAL 12 SHOWS, THERE WAS, THANKS TO WHEDON'S CAREFUL PLANNING, AN ENDING OF SORTS TO THE SERIES. THANKFULLY, IT WASN'T NECESSARY.

Naturally, the Judge doesn't survive long in the episode, as Buffy botches things up for the vampires. In fact, there's a humorous bit where Spike suggests they leave Sunnydale because nothing seems to work for them the way it's supposed to. The vamp's got a point there.

Big moment: Angel and Buffy declare their love for each other and finally make love. Of course, these kids should have seen one or two horror movies in their lives. Don't they know that premarital sex usually leads to something horrible? Well, it certainly does here. The way that Angel's curse is designed, at the moment he achieves true happiness, his soul is taken from him again and he becomes a creature of pure evil. Guess they call it forbidden love for a reason.

The choreography of the fights is great, and this is one area at which the show continues to excel. You would probably be hard-pressed to find another series with fisticuffs action scenes that work as effectively as they do on *Buffy*.

Despite the episode ending with a cliffhanger, much of the action serves as a build-up to the conclusion. Usually, part one of a series two-parter represents an ever-escalating chain of events that part two must somehow wrap up. As strong as this episode is, there's really not a hell of a lot going on—though, surprisingly, that doesn't take away from its strengths. Overall, it's a perfect example of how *Buffy* is a show that improves as it goes on.

Episode Twenty-Six: "Innocence"

Original Airdate: 1/20/98
Written and Directed by Joss Whedon
Guest Starring Seth Green (Oz), Kristine Sutherland (Joyce Summers), Robia La Morte (Ms. Calendar), Brian Thompson (The Judge), Ryan Francis (Soldier), Vincent Schiavelli (Jenny's Uncle), James Marsters (Spike), Juliet Landau (Drusilla), James Lurie (Teacher), Carla Madden (Woman), Parry Shen (Student)

PRESS SYNOPSIS After Buffy shares an intimate moment with Angel that extinguishes his human soul, she is left with the realization that she must destroy the now-evil Angel who has transformed into his previous persona of Angelus. Meanwhile, Giles's relationship with Jenny Calendar (recurring star Robia La Morte) takes on a new twist when he discovers that she is a member of the Gypsy family who gave Angel his human soul, and Willow's hopes of a relationship with Xander are dashed when she discovers Xander and Cordelia's secret romance.

COMMENTARY (✝✝✝½) In many interviews, *Buffy* creator/executive producer Joss Whedon has argued the virtues of television over movies, and each time he serves as both writer and director he proves just how much can be accomplished within the limited budget of a weekly television show. In his more than capable hands, a series episode takes on a cinematic flavor with increasingly intense action sequences, yet it never loses sight of the characters.

The episode begins with Angel going bonkers in the aftermath of making love with Buffy. He bites the neck of a woman who has just taken a drag on a cigarette, and when her body drops out of frame, *Angel* lets out the smoke. An inspired moment. You don't see things like that on most TV shows.

Our fascination with this episode comes from watching David Boreanaz sink to a new low in evildoing, which, for the actor, must have been a relief after playing mysterious and moody nice guy Angel throughout the first two seasons. He's obviously relishing the opportunity presented to him, and he brings his scenes to life in ways he was unable to do before (and that's not even a slam; he was fine before, but the character wasn't very extraordinary). It begins with his being absolutely cruel to Buffy, criticizing her performance in bed and basically admitting that he told her he loved her just so they would have sex. Once again, Sarah Michelle Gellar does a great job, really capturing and conveying the pain that Buffy feels in this kind of situation, questioning everything that's happened and feeling completely inadequate. Later, after Angel has let Spike and Drusilla see the "new" him, he notes, "Buffy made me feel like a human being. . . . Some things you don't forgive."

His cruelty continues, as he kills Calendar's uncle and writes, in blood, on the wall, "Was it good for you, too?" This leads Giles to note that Angel is making it harder for Buffy to function. Her response is, "No, he's making it easier for me to kill him."

Great third act scene: A mall in Sunnydale is the locale as the resurrected Judge and a bazillion vampires decide to claim some souls. The Judge is zapping shoppers when Buffy interrupts him with a crossbow to the heart—which only serves to irritate him. But *then* in a wild, almost over-the-top moment, she picks up a bazooka stolen from a local armory and fires, blowing the unexpected Judge to pieces. Then, with the episode going from strength to strength, the situation turns into a one-on-one fight between Buffy and Angel, but she can't bring herself to stake him. Angel taunts her until she kicks him in his undead jewels, which has the same effect on him that it would on humans. Yet another way to harm a vampire, and you don't even need a priest to bless anything.

Cool moment #1: Angel has Willow in his arms and is about to kill her, when Xander, armed with a cross, performs an effective rescue.

Cool moment #2: Buffy learns the truth about Ms. Calendar. She rushes into school, enters the classroom *while* class is in session, slams Ms. Calendar

back on a desk, and demands an explanation. They never did *this* on *90210*.

A terrific show, but one that also spoils the viewer in terms of more mundane high school analogy episodes.

Episode Twenty-Seven: "Phases"

Original Airdate: 1/27/98
Written by Rob Des Hotel and Dean Batali
Directed by Bruce Seth Green
Guest Starring Seth Green (Oz), Camila Griggs (Gym Teacher), Jack Conley (Cain), Larry Bagby III (Larry), Megahn Perry (Theresa Klusmeyer), Keith Campbell (Werewolf)

PRESS SYNOPSIS When a werewolf descends upon the city of Sunnydale, it is up to Buffy (Sarah Michelle Gellar) and the gang to protect the mostly human being from an evil poacher (guest star Jack Conley) who is hunting the animal for sport. Meanwhile, much to Xander's (Nicholas Brendon) dismay, Willow (Alyson Hannigan) turns her romantic interests to Oz (guest star

Seth Green), unaware of the danger she is about to face.

COMMENTARY (✝✝½) Well, it was only a matter of time before a werewolf raised its furry head at Sunnydale. The arrival was inevitable, but the pleasant twist came from the fact that it wasn't a monster of the week but instead a character we had already gotten to know a bit. Guest star Seth Green does a great job as the very cool, pretty much un-flappable Oz. Despite the rather low-budget approach to his makeup as the werewolf, the actor manages to be real in the scenes, and that's all you can ask for in such a situation.

Some good character bits, most no-tably the comfort zone that's starting to be reached between Cordelia and Xander, with the former once again proving how far she has come from the empty-headed bimbo of season one. Both Charisma Carpenter and Nich-olas Brendon play off each other ex-ceptionally well, and it will be interest-ing to see where they go with this. The same can be said for Alyson Hannigan

and Seth Green—particularly at epi-sode's end when Willow makes it clear that she accepts him even if he does bay at the full moon.

If there's anything disappointing about the episode, it's just that it has really jumped into *Dark Shadows* terri-tory. While yours truly is one of the greatest supporters of continuity you could ever find, there comes a point where things really start to go nutso. For instance, you've got the character Oz, a werewolf, staring at the cheer-leading trophy of Catherine Madison (from season one's "The Witch"), a witch trapped in the body of the tro-phy, and later on doing battle with vampires. Is it just me, or is there something kind of crazy about this?

Speaking of continuity, there's a nice bit of it relating to the previous two-parter in which the vampire Theresa approaches Buffy and tells her that Angel sends his love, a state-ment that just rips her apart. Not to worry, though, because Theresa ulti-mately gets the point (pun definitely intended).

Episode Twenty-Eight: "Bewitched, Bothered, and Bewildered"

Original Airdate: 2/10/98
Written by Marti Noxon
Directed by James A. Contner
Guest Starring Seth Green (Oz), Kristine Sutherland (Joyce Summers), Robia La Morte (Ms. Calendar), Elizabeth Anne Allen (Amy), Merches McNab (Harmony), Lorna Scott (Miss Beakman), James Marsters (Spike), Juliet Landau (Drusilla), Jason Hall (Devon), Jennie Chester (Kate), Kristen Winnicki (Cordette), Tamara Braun (Frenzied Girl), Scott Hamm (Jock)

PRESS SYNOPSIS When Cordelia succumbs to peer pressure and breaks off her tryst with Xander on Valentine's Day, he convinces a witch (guest star Elizabeth Anne Allen) to put a spell on Cordelia that will make her fall in love with him. But when the spell backfires, the women in Sunnydale, except for Cordelia and including Buffy and Drusilla (recurring star Juliet Landau), begin to see Xander in a whole new light.

COMMENTARY (✝✝½) An amusing standalone episode that takes the old-fashioned notion of a love potion and tweaks it in such a way as to make it feel different from other similar storylines.

What really drives the episode are the legitimate emotions behind the actions of Xander and Cordelia. Her breaking up with him because of peer pressure strikes a chord because it's real, and his responding anger and frustration are something that many a high-schooler can identity with; and thanks to Amy (Elizabeth Anne Allen), he has the means of striking back. It's a bit unappealing for Xander to want to make Cordelia fall in love with him so that he can break up with her and show her what it feels like, and it's also a little more malicious than we're used to from the character. The fact that things work out alright in the end for the two of them (and Charisma Carpenter shines in the moment when Cordelia tells off her friends regarding Xander) apparently makes it all worthwhile.

Structurally, the episode manages to segue back and forth between humor and horror, the former in terms of everyone but Cordelia coming on to Xander, including Buffy (who even strips to seduce him!), Willow, Ms. Calendar, Mrs. Summers, and Drusilla. Humor is also mined from Amy, another adoring member of the Xander Fan Club, who uses her witchcraft to turn the Slayer into a rat. The horror elements kick in when these possessed women start going to extremes (i.e., Willow walking around with an axe, threatening the competition; Cordelia finding herself the victim of a lynch mob, etc.).

Dopey point: Given that Amy had the experience she did in season one's "The Witch," why on earth would she pick up where her mother left off in terms of witchcraft? It seems a highly unlikely point.

Basically, a straight ball down the middle kind of show.

Episode Twenty-Nine: "Passion"

Original Airdate: 2/24/98
Written by Ty King

Directed by Michael Gershman
Guest Starring Kristine Sutherland (Joyce Summers), Robia La Morte (Ms. Calendar), Richard Assad (Shopkeeper), James Marsters (Spike), Juliet Landau (Drusilla), Danny Strong (Jonathan)

PRESS SYNOPSIS   Angel's obsession with tormenting Buffy takes a dangerous turn when he starts edging closer to her heart—and home—forcing Buffy to have a serious talk with her mom (Kristine Sutherland). Meanwhile, Jenny (Robia La Morte) is doing everything in her power to right her wrongs, especially the one with Giles.

COMMENTARY (✝✝✝✝)   Good lord, it doesn't get any better than this. Writer Ty King and director Michael Gershman deserve credit for out-Jossing Joss Whedon and giving us an episode that is easily the best one yet of the series. What's amazing is that the been there—done that *X-Files* will undoubtedly get yet another Emmy nomination for best drama, but this episode of *Buffy* blows away just about everything else that show has done for the past two seasons.

THE FIGHT SEQUENCES ARE EXTREMELY WELL-CHOREOGRAPHED, WITH AN INTENSITY THAT MANY OF THE PREVIOUS FIGHTS HAD NEVER ACHIEVED: GELLAR COMES ACROSS MORE LIKE RAMBO THAN BUFFY. IN ALL LIKELIHOOD, GELLAR, IN A SUMMER WHEN SHE WAS FORCED TO PLAY A VICTIM IN MOVIES, PROBABLY ENJOYED THE OPPORTUNITY TO KICK SOME ASS INSTEAD.

As always, the teaser is terrific fun: coming out of the Bronze, Buffy, Willow, Xander, and Cordelia walk by a couple "necking." As soon as they've passed, Angel drops the body of his latest victim and watches them walk away.

The strength comes from Angel's continuing efforts to torment Buffy.

He goes into her room while she's sleeping, strokes her hair gently (seeming to possess benevolent feelings for her, though it isn't likely), and leaves a present for her to wake up to—a portrait he's sketched of her. From there, he kills Willow's fish and leaves them on a hook in an envelope.

Check out Gellar's bitchy performance as she virtually ignores Ms. Calendar, whom she holds at least partially responsible for what's happened to Angel. Ms. Calendar actually does manage to gain some sympathy, telling Giles that loyalty to her people was the first thing she was taught. In the same conversation, she also slips in the bombshell that she has fallen in love with him.

Comparative observation: Every time Drusilla gets a premonition, she seems to double over in pain. Perhaps she is actually doing an impersonation of Marina Sirtis's Counselor Troi ("Ugh . . . Captain, I feel pain") from the early days of *Star Trek: The Next Generation*.

Cool moment: Angel tells Mrs. Summers that he and Buffy slept together, and he's about to follow the woman into the house when he suddenly finds that he can no longer enter. Buffy and Willow have performed a revocation chant that has essentially "uninvited" him into her home.

The best scenes of the episode involve Angel finding Ms. Calendar in school, where she is working on a way to give the curse back to him, thus returning his soul. He trashes the computer room (missing a backup disk containing the necessary information—a red herring for a future episode), then begins a really intense game of cat-and-mouse. It concludes with a shocking moment when Angel grabs her, snaps her neck, drops the woman to the floor, and cracks a joke. But, wait, there's more: later, Giles comes home, finds candles lit all over the place, music playing, and a note that says, "Upstairs." Delighted, he

heads there, his joy rapidly turning to terror when he finds Calendar's dead body in his bed. From this moment on, you're made aware that *Buffy the Vampire Slayer* ain't taking no prisoners!

Episode Thirty: "Killed by Death"

Original Airdate: 3/3/98
Written by Rob Des Hotel and Dean Batali
Directed by Deren Sarafian
Guest Starring Kristine Sutherland (Joyce Summers), Richard Herd (Dr. Stanley Backer), Willie Garson (Security Guard), Andrew Ducote (Ryan), Juanita Jennings (Dr. Wilkinson), Robert Munic (Intern), Mimi Paley (Little Buffy), Denise Johnson (Celia), James Jude Courtney (Der Kindestod)

PRESS SYNOPSIS Buffy is admitted to the hospital with a raging fever; there she encounters a young child (guest star Andrew Ducote) who brings with him nightmares of Buffy's past and present. Meanwhile, a jealous Cordelia looks on as Xander protects a weakened Buffy from Angel's fury.

COMMENTARY (✝✝½) Pretty much a straight-ahead Bogeyman episode, which works fairly well although some elements seem reminiscent of the *Nightmare on Elm Street* film series.

What does work about the show—and this is really a testament to how much emotional power can be generated from the more suggestive elements of horror rather than out-and-out gore—are certain moments when people seem to be fighting phantoms (although the phantoms are not shown to us). We see a doctor, perceived to be a threat by the Freddy Krueger–wannabe, viciously attacked by an unseen presence, his body thrown around the hospital room, gashes mysteriously appearing on his body as he is being pummeled and then dragged away. There's an even more impressive moment told via flashback when Buffy's cousin was in a hospital and let out a bloodcurdling scream while she swatted at the air, apparently to get away from *something*. It's a terrific performance, made completely real.

Buffy's discovery that she has to be feverish to battle this demon is okay, albeit a bit silly. Actually, it's somewhat reminiscent of an episode of *Buck Rogers in the 25th Century*, in which Gil Gerard's Buck, who is stuck in sickbay because of a fever, is the only person who can see an alien assassin.

Good character stuff: We see that Buffy is deathly afraid of hospitals because of what happened to her cousin, and Cordelia expresses her jealousy over Xander's constant concern for Buffy.

Perhaps this episode would have been perceived differently had it not come after the raw power of "Passion."

Guest star note: Richard Herd, who portrayed Dr. Stanley Backer, also portrayed the Supreme Leader "John" in the original *"V"* miniseries and its followup, *"V"—The Final Battle*.

Episode Thirty-One: "I Only Have Eyes for You"

Original Airdate: 4/28/98
Written by Marti Noxon
Directed by James Whitmore, Jr.

Guest Starring Meredith Salinger (Grace Newman), Christopher Gorham (James Stanley), John Hawkes (George), Miriam Flynn (Ms. Frank), Brian Reddy (Policeman Bob), James Marsters (Spike), Juliet Landau (Drusilla), Armin Shimerman (Principal Snyder), Brian Poth (Fighting Boy), Sarah Bibb (Fighting Girl), James Lurie (Mr. Miller), Ryan Taszreak (Ben), Anna Coman-Hidy (Fifties Girl #1), Vanessa Bodnar (Fifties Girl #2)

PRESS SYNOPSIS Buffy encounters a tortured spirit haunting the halls of Sunnydale High and recruits her friends to help the bitter spirit in its quest for peace. Meanwhile, Giles is filled with anguish when he believes the spiritual being is Jenny, trapped and trying to impart a final message to him from the beyond.

COMMENTARY (✝✝½) Possession is a theme that *Buffy* hasn't really dealt with, and it's handled well in this story of a doomed love from the 1950s in which a student killed his teacher when she was about to break off their affair.

While the storyline is nothing too special, what makes it work so well is the subtext of the characters. The ghost of James, the student, is seeking forgiveness from the spirit of his teacher, and it's something that only Buffy, Giles, and the gang can help with. But Buffy, given her situation with Angel, has no forgiveness for him; she doesn't think redemption should be given.

The heart of the show comes at the conclusion, though, when Buffy and Angel—who has been goaded on by Spike to take his battle to Buffy—are possessed by the spirits of the doomed lovers and, unfortunately, are forced to replay the tragic events of the past all over again. The difference, though, is that Angel's body can't really be killed and the spirit of the teacher, Ms. Newman, tells Buffy/James that she does indeed forgive him. The lovers kiss, freeing their spirits from Sunnydale and leaving Buffy and Angel at very close quarters. Angel freaks and furiously leaves.

The most annoying aspect of this episode is the police conferring with

Snyder, alluding to the fact that they know about the Hellmouth and need to keep it a secret. Let's get something straight here, fellows: *Buffy* is not *The X-Files,* and any attempt to laden the series with that show's grand conspiracy theme only serves to cheapen what is usually one of the most unique visions on television. Be happy with that, will you?

Episode Thirty-Two: "Go Fish"

Original Airdate: 5/5/98
Written by David Fury and Elin Hampton
Directed by David Semel
Guest Starring Armin Shimerman (Principal Snyder), Charles Cyphers (Coach Marin), Jeremy Garrett (Cameron Walker), Wentworth Miller (Gage Petronzi), Conchata Ferrell (Nurse Greenliech), Danny Strong (Jonathan), Shane West (Sean), Jake Patellis (Dodd McAlvy)

PRESS SYNOPSIS When a monster starts preying on members of the high school swim team, Buffy takes it upon herself to become the protector of the star players. Meanwhile, Xander goes undercover to discover the truth about the missing teammates and ends up revealing a rarely seen side of himself.

COMMENTARY (✝½) Pretty much the worst episode of the series so far, combining elements of *The Creature from the Black Lagoon, The X-Files's* episode "The Host," and a public service message ("Boys and girls, steroids are bad!"). As always, Nicholas Brendon does his best to make things credible, but it just feels like a filler episode, as if everyone were taking an emotional break after all the crap they'd been through this season and were only focused on preparing for the two-part season finale.

Episode Thirty-Three: "Becoming, Part 1"

Original Airdate: 5/12/98
Written and Directed by Joss Whedon
Guest Starring Seth Green (Oz), Kristine Sutherland (Joyce Summers), Julie Benz (Darla), Bianca Lawson (Kendra), Jack McGee (Doug Perren), Richard Riehle (Buffy's First Watcher), James Marsters

(Spike), Juliet Landau (Drusilla), Armin Shimerman (Principal Snyder), Shannon Weller (Gypsy Woman), Zitto Kazann (Gypsy Man), Ginger Williams (Girl)

PRESS SYNOPSIS A web of conspiracy, suspense, and heartbreak surround the second season finale of *Buffy the Vampire Slayer*. Buffy determines that the time has come to destroy Angel and must ascertain if she is ready to sacrifice all she knows to be true to do so, but her decision is further entangled when Willow uncovers the secret that may restore Buffy's former beloved. Elsewhere, Angel chooses to unearth an evil demon that could swallow the earth and all of its beings, rather than return to the arms of his former lover.

COMMENTARY (✝✝✝½) The episode begins with Angel's narration, which was the case with "Passion" as well—implying that if the character does indeed get his own series, which is the rumor at the time this book is going to press, Angel's narration could be a feature of that show.

The design of much of this episode provides us with some idea of Angel's origin. It begins with flashbacks that are sparse in production value but effective. In one flashback, we see Angel screwing over the still-human Drusilla while she's in church, confessing that she is having evil thoughts. Angel, sitting in for the priest, tells her she should give in to her evil, but she valiantly tries to avoid that, attempting to hold on to the values of the church. A neat, albeit cruel, scene, but it does raise two questions: how is Angel, a vampire, in a church in the first place, and how is he interacting with Drusilla with the sun shining brightly in the sky?

Other flashbacks chronicle Angel's being turned into a vampire in the first place, the Gypsy curse being placed on him, and the resulting guilt he suddenly feels for all of the victims he's claimed over the course of a century. Angel is carrying a hell of a lot of emotional baggage with him, as it's revealed.

In a sense, Ms. Calendar gets the opportunity to redeem herself from beyond the grave when Willow and Buffy find the computer disk with the restoration ritual on it. This does, however, lead to an interesting debate in which Xander makes it clear that Angel should be killed for the murders he's committed, while Buffy and the others feel that if there is a chance for redemption it should be taken. Two sides of an argument, and both of them are right.

In a 1996 flashback, Angel roams the streets of New York as a homeless person, feeding on an occasional rat. A demon named Whistler, who supposedly serves as a balance between the realms of good and evil, takes him under his arm and gets him to turn his life around. Doing so takes them to Los Angeles, where Angel catches sight of Buffy at her first high school. This is amusing, as Gellar is a Valley Girl in full force and every bit as vacuous as Cordelia used to be. We're also given the opportunity to see events from the movie restaged with the actress, though these sequences are terribly marred by Richard Riehle being cast in Donald Sutherland's role. No one expects them to get Sutherland to do the show, but to go with an actor who is *so* different is actually distracting. What is interesting about the scene, though, is that Angel studies Buffy and sees her as someone he would like to help someday.

What actually hurts this episode a bit is the vampires' plot to raise the demon that will plunge the world into the Apocalypse. The truth is, the idea of resurrecting this demon or that one is really starting to become old hat (attempts to revive the Master, the Judge, etc.). There's also the growing problem of Buffy struggling with studying and school in general, which are issues that seem incredibly mundane compared to the ongoing story arc.

There's a cool battle between Buffy and Angel, designed to be a distraction from events at the library where vampires have invaded, Giles is taken prisoner, Xander's arm is broken, and the returning Kendra the Vampire Slayer battles Drusilla and is killed for her trouble. Most of this is really great, but Kendra proves to be so useless that one wonders why she was brought back at all, except maybe to ultimately make Buffy alone in her quest. For a woman who has spent her entire life training to slay vampires, she's pretty ineffectual.

Joss Whedon delivers a real bionic moment when Buffy enters the school at full speed, and in midstride she goes into slow motion. Quite effective, as is the resulting moment when the police arrive and point guns at Buffy, thinking she's responsible for the deaths around her.

Although this is a strong episode, it doesn't seem to display Whedon's usual high standards, part of the problem being the episode's slightly meandering pace. When it works, there's no stopping it; otherwise, it's a slightly above-average show.

Episode Thirty-Four: "Becoming, Part 2"

Original Airdate: 5/19/98
Written and Directed by Joss Whedon
Guest Starring Max Perlich (Whistler), Seth Green (Oz), Kristine Sutherland (Joyce Summers), Robia La Morte (Ms. Calendar), James G. MacDonald (Police Detective), James Marsters (Spike), Juliet Landau (Drusilla), Armin Shimerman

(Principal Snyder), Susan Leslie (First Cop), Thomas G. Waites (Second Cop)

PRESS SYNOPSIS The suspense continues as Hell prepares to swallow the world and Buffy is left alone to stop it. With Giles in the hands of the enemy and Angel primed for destruction, our Slayer is forced into some treacherous alliances and is faced with life-changing decisions.

COMMENTARY (✝✝✝✝) In the teaser, Buffy breaks free from the cops *and* gets to call Principal Snyder a "stupid little troll." Now *that's* a teaser.

Initially, the episode is dealing with the aftermath of the battle from part one: Willow is in a coma, suffering from head trauma; Xander's arm is in a cast; and Giles has been taken prisoner by Angel, who needs help in resurrecting the demon.

There are indeed strange alliances in this episode. First, Buffy meets up with Whistler, who offers some helpful hints, and then Spike(!) shows up with a deal: if Buffy helps him get rid of Angel, he and Drusilla will leave

Sunnydale never to return. It seems that Spike's not enjoying how much time Angel and Dru are spending together, and he's incapable of stopping it himself. There's an amusing moment when the partnership is being formed, in which Spike admits that he doesn't want the world to go to Hell; that he likes people—"they're like Happy Meals with legs." Very cute.

Trouble for Buffy, in that mom catches her in action and Buffy has to finally confess that she's a Vampire Slayer, which is all initially played pretty droll and matter of factly. It's humorous but a little out of place, what with Giles being tortured by Angel and all. Eventually, it becomes much more serious and real, though it ends kind of dopey, with mom shouting, "If you walk out of this house, don't even think about coming back."

Things go from bad to worse for Buffy on a personal level when she goes back to the library to retrieve a mystical sword to battle the demon, and Principal Snyder catches and expels her (it's amazing who you'll find in a high school library after hours).

There's a cool bit where Drusilla, after Angel hasn't had much luck, approaches the tied-up Giles and tells him to see with his heart. Suddenly, she is transformed into Ms. Calendar and she pumps him for information. It's a gut-wrenching moment for Giles, who ultimately tells her that Angel's own blood is what will allow the portal to Hell to open. Angel ultimately cuts his hand, wiping the blood on the statue of a demon, and has to wait for the vortex to begin.

In the meantime, Buffy learns from Whistler that Angel's blood is also the thing that will send both Angel and the demon back to Hell. This leads to an incredible battle between Buffy and Angel, and, surprisingly, Drusilla and Spike after she realizes Spike's betrayal. This is successfully intercut with scenes of the now-awake Willow (who has picked up where techno-pagan Ms. Calendar left off) leading the gang in the restoration ritual.

The third act of the show seems like a foregone conclusion. While Buffy and Angel are fighting with swords (giving the show a positively *Highlander* feel), the audience just knows that Angel will get his soul back at the very last second—and he does. What comes across as a complete surprise, however, is that just as Buffy realizes her old Angel is back, the portal to Hell opens up. It is an incredibly tense and moving moment when they declare their love for each other, Buffy tells him to close his eyes, and then she thrusts the mystical sword through him and into the demon, catapulting them both into Hell.

Give credit to both Gellar and Boreanaz for pulling this off so successfully. You feel her anguish, and you see the utter confusion on Angel's face as he vanishes. Just an incredible moment of television.

As the episode ends, the Buffy "universe" is thrust into disarray, with Buffy leaving Sunnydale behind her for destinations unknown. Just as he did at the conclusion of season one, Joss Whedon has set the show up in such a way that if it doesn't come back for a third year, it will still have had a conclusion of sorts.

What happens next is anybody's guess, but given the way that *Buffy the Vampire Slayer* has continued to evolve and grow beyond even the most optimistic critic's expectations, one can assume that Whedon has quite a number of surprises in store for the audience.

He'd better . . . or else.

CHAPTER FIVE

SLAYER RESOURCES

BUFFY, THE VAMPIRE SLAYER

Official Buffy the Vampire Slayer Web Page

http://www.buffyslayer.com/home.html

Angel's Buffy the Vampire Slayer Page

http://www.geocities.com/Hollywood/Theater/5261/opening.html

Angelus' Buffy the Vampire Slayer Page

http://www.geocities.com/TelevisionCity/8179/

Beth's Buffy Page

http://www.geocities.com/Hollywood/Makeup/6497/

Buff-a-Maniacs

http:www.geocities.com/Hollywood/Theater/4051/index.html

Buffy Cross & Stake

http://members.aol.com/aglx/main.html

Buffy's Domain of Delight

http://www.angelfire.com/hi/buffyrules/

Buffy Lover

http://www.geocities.com/Hollywood/Boulevard/1099/

SLAYER RESOURCES

Buffy the Chosen One

http://www.geocities.com/Hollywood/Theater/7275/

Buffy the Vampire Slayer Central

http://www.koganuts.com/IGalleries/Btvs/index.html

Buffy the Vampire Slayer Fan Page

http://www.geocities.com/TelevisionCity/Studio/2787/

Buffy the Vampire Slayer: Obsession

http://www.geocities.com/Television/Studio/2787/

Buffy: Vampire Slaying Goddess

http://www.geocities.com/TelevisionCity/5946/

Domain of the Slain

http://www2.uic.edu/~ahufan1/btvs/

Got Stakes?

http://www.geocities.com/Hollywood/Makeup/2857/Buffy.htm

Punch's Buffy the Vampire Slayer Page

http://www.geocities.com/TelevisionCity/Set/108/index.html

Raven's Realm of Buffy the Vampire Slayer

http://www.geocities.com/Area51/Chamber/3821/buffy.html

Rodrigo's Buffy Page

http://www.cenweb.com/rodrigo/

Slayer's Lair

http://www.geocities.com/Hollywood/Set/7517/

The Sanctum

http://members.tripod.com/~The Sanctum/

The Slayer's Diaries

http://www.geocities.com/Hollywood/Theater/6331/

The Sounds of the Slayer

http://techsero.simplenet.com/buffy/

UK Buffy Page

http://www.hedgehog.demon.co.uk/buffy/

Ultimate Buffy the Vampire Slayer Page

http://members.aol.com/Hacker409/buffyslayer.html

SARAH MICHELLE GELLAR

Absolute Sarah

http://wildrOid.interspeed.net/

Bob's Sarah Michelle Gellar Page

http://www.geocities.com/TelevisionCity/1549.htm

Illuminations of Sarah Michelle Gellar

http://www.geocities.com/Hollywood/Lot/2535/

Sarah Michelle Gellar!

http://members.tripod.com/~Grassfire/SMG.html

Sarah Michelle Gellar: Brighter Than Any Star

http://www.sarah-michelle-gellar.com/

Sarah Michelle Gellar Fan Page

http://www.smgfan.com/

Sarah Michelle Gellar Pics Page

http://www.geocities.com/TelevisionCity/9169

Sarah Michelle Gellar Unveiled

http://www.geocities.com/Hollywood/Boulevard/9800/smg.html

Sarah Online

http://aj.simplenet.com/smg_world/main.html

Visions of Sarah Michelle Gellar

http://rc.simplenet.com/smg_page/

DAVID BOREANAZ

Angel of the Night

http://www.members.aol.com/AutumnSun/Angel.html

Angel's Apartment

http://members.tripod.com/~Angelis444/index-7.html

Heaven's Gates

http://www.geocities.com/SoHo/Cafe/3863

The Angel Keepers Page

http://www.geocities.com/Hollywood/Academy/4949/angel-list.html

NICHOLAS BRENDON

Babe Known As Xander

http://xander.interspeed.net/index2.html

Yet Still More Nicholas Brendon Mania!!

http://members.aol.com/rbsayre/xander.html

ALYSON HANNIGAN

Alyson Hannigan Appreciation Society

http://www.network23.com/hub/ahas/

The Alyson Hannigan Altar

http://users.twave.net/shrine/ahaltar.htm

Willow Web

http://www.students.bucknell.edu/rfaust/willow/

Wonderful Willow

http://www.geocities.com/TelevisionCity/Set/6710/home.html

CHARISMA CARPENTER

Charisma Carpenter

http://www.geocities.com/TelevisionCity/Set/3954/center.html

ANTHONY STEWART HEAD

The Official Giles' Appreciation Society Panters Home Page

http://www.geocities.com/TelevisionCity/7728/gaspers.html

JULIET LANDAU AND JAMES MARSTERS

A Home for Dru and Spike

http://www.geocities.com/Vienna/Strasse/4731/index.html

Drusilla's Dollhouse

http://www.angelfire.com/wa/Drusilla/

Dru and Spike's Domain

http://www.angelfire.com/sd/druspike/index.html

Spike and Drusilla

http://www.geocities.com/Area51/Shire/5062/

Spike and Drusilla's Vampire Queendome

http://www.angelfire.com/va/drusilla/

USENET

alt.tv.buffy-v-slayer

alt.tv.buffy-v-slayer.creative

Albert L. Ortega

Albert L. Ortega

Albert L. Ortega

Albert L. Ortega

Albert L. Ortega

Albert L. Ortega

THE *DARK SHADOWS* CONNECTION

THE SERIES

While it's not unusual for a dream to be the basis of someone's goals, it's not so common for it to serve as the foundation of a phenomenon that touched millions. Such was reportedly the case with Dan Curtis and the creation of *Dark Shadows,* the world's only Gothic horror soap opera, which ran on ABC from 1966 to 1971.

"I awoke suddenly in the middle of a strange dream," Curtis explains. "The bedroom was pitch black, yet I could see the dream clearly. My dream was about a girl riding on a train. She was reading a letter and gazing out the window."

He explains that a voice-over said that she had been hired as a governess at an old place (which would eventually become Collinwood) along the New England seacoast. The dream ended with the girl standing at a deserted station in the middle of the night as the train pulled away.

"I forced myself to come awake and lit a cigarette," he reminisces. "I thought about it and it was brilliantly logical to me."

The next day he told ABC about his dream and they expressed interest in turning it into a soap opera. The network gave Curtis a budget and proceeded to turn his dream into reality.

"Yes, that was his famed dream," says Sam Hall, one of the head writers for the series, "but Dan mostly did *Dark Shadows* because he wanted millions of dollars."

As Hall explains it, Curtis had started out selling time for MCA, when, because of his love for the sport, he thought of putting throat mikes on golfers "so you could hear them say 'shit' when they missed," he smiles. "He sold that to CBS and it was called *CBS Golf Classics.*"

The program won an Emmy Award in 1965 and further filled Curtis's streak of independence, causing him to remark that he was "sick of selling other people's garbage."

A man always ready to move on to other things, Curtis got bored with the show and decided that soap operas made the most money. Shortly thereafter, Curtis's dream was given life, and he went about the task of obtaining a cast and crew. A member of the latter was Art Wallace, who had been a professional singer and was taking voice lessons under the American Theater wing, when he decided to take a course on writing for television. A script he had written for the course sold to a television series called *The Web.*

"It was live television," explains Wallace. "After that script, they asked me how many I could write in a month. It was a weekly show, a half-hour anthological suspense series. After that, I just kept on writing for different shows."

Several years later, Dan Curtis came to him and said that he had a commitment to develop a new daytime show for ABC. He had interested them in doing a Gothic show, although he didn't know what that show would be.

"He wanted to know if I would be interested in producing it," says the writer. "I told him that I wouldn't, but I might be interested in writing and creating it. I had written a one-hour movie for *Studio One,* a very prestigious anthology series. My script, called 'The House,' was about a woman who hadn't left the house in twenty years, and it was very much like the beginnings of *Dark Shadows.* I used 'The House' as a basis for developing all the characters that were on the show in the beginning. I wrote a bible for the show, and ABC decided to go ahead with it."

It's mentioned that Curtis purports to have created the show from a dream.

"What came to him in a dream, if it was a dream," Wallace counters, "was the idea of doing a Gothic show, but he had no show. He just had the idea of doing a daytime serial which would be different. He had no characters, no story, no nothing. The idea of doing a Gothic show is what interested the network. Now if Dan Curtis dreamed that, then it's fine with me. I wrote the show, creating the actual details. For the first thirteen weeks of the show, I wrote the whole thing, sixty-five scripts.

"Part of the situation," he continues, "in negotiating the contract I had with him, he insisted that he wanted to be called the creator of the show, and we went head to head because he didn't create the show, I did. He was totally adamant, so we finally arrived at the conclusion that the credits would read, 'Series Created by Dan Curtis. Story Created and Developed by Art Wallace.' That was just in order to get the contract completed, because he just refused to give up that credit. I would say that this credit should have said, 'Concept by Dan Curtis.' But he wanted that. So I wrote the first thirteen weeks of the show, and after I had done that I found myself getting kind of slap happy. We brought in other writers, and I just kind of supervised."

Curtis next tried to come up with a title for the series. He considered "Terror at Collinwood," "Castle of Darkness," and "The House on Widow's Hill," before finally latching onto *Dark Shadows.*

"The next thing I had to do," Curtis recalls, "was to find a house that could be Collinwood. I sent teams of researchers into the field, but I myself discovered the house we actually used."

Exteriors of the brooding 40-room mansion were shot in Newport, Rhode Island, while footage of Barnabas Collins's Old House was obtained in Tarrytown, New York; and Essex, Connecticut, doubled for the town of Collinsport, Maine.

Hopes were high for the show, but no one—not even Curtis—could have foreseen the phenomenon it would become.

Gathering the Creative Hands

Dan Curtis began to assemble the crew necessary to bring *Dark Shadows* to the air, starting with producer Robert Costello.

"In 1966, I heard a new show was being formed," Costello says, "and was told that they were looking for a producer, because the guy who created it, Dan Curtis, had only done golf shows. He knew nothing about producing a dramatic show. We met, liked each other, and joined with a friend of mine, Art Wallace, who had developed it with Dan and was writing the series."

Two alternating directors were chosen: Lela Swift and John Sedwick, who, like Costello, had a theatrical background but ended up in television on such shows as *The Nurses* and *Confidential*. Finally, Robert Cobert was pegged as composer (his main title theme remains one of the eeriest on television) and Sy Tomashoff as scenic designer, a role he excelled in, as can be witnessed by the extraordinary sets he created in the studio.

Curtis next turned his attention to casting, claiming that he "wanted somebody with class" to portray Elizabeth Collins Stoddard, the matriarch of Collinwood. He found that somebody in the form of veteran actress Joan Bennett.

"What I really wanted was a play on Broadway," says Bennett, "but it gets very depressing for an actor to just sit around. With my children grown, I was going stir crazy. I had never looked at a soap opera in my life, and I thought they all had rotten actors. I was surprised to find good actors here."

Louis Edmonds was signed as Elizabeth's brother, Roger Collins; David Henesy portrayed his son, David; Nancy Barrett was Elizabeth's daughter, Carolyn; Alexandra Moltke (now Isles) personified Curtis's dream as Victoria Winters, the mysterious girl on the train; and Kathryn Leigh Scott played Maggie Evans, a local waitress.

With cast and crew in place, *Dark Shadows* began taping in mid-1966 in nearly living black and white (though a transition to color would occur about a year into its run) and differed from other soaps in that it didn't focus on standard topics such as extramarital sex or unwed mothers, but rather on more "Gothic" themes. There were things that went bump in the night, hidden panels, and an occasional ghost. ("We did two ghost stories before the vampire arrived," Curtis declares.)

The intertwining of the lives of the people at Collinwood filled the show's early months, and the audience really didn't seem to care.

"The show was limping along, really limping," writer Sam Hall relates, "and ABC said, 'We're canceling it. Unless you pick up in twenty-six weeks, you're finished.' Dan had always wanted to do a vampire picture, so he decided to bring a vampire on the series."

Recalls writer Ron Sproat, "We were having a cousin coming from England. It was another blackmail plot that had been projected, and Dan Curtis said, 'I want to go for broke. I want a vampire in there.' I loved it and thought it was terrific. The only concern I voiced was, 'What are we going to do to top it?' It's real exciting and fun and I love vampires, but I just couldn't think of anything we could do after that which would top it. As it turned out, though, he stayed on the show until the end. At any rate, we did it and Dan said this was Russian Roulette. So we went with it and had lots of story meetings. I remember one meeting that lasted twenty-seven hours, because we were fighting deadlines and making this stuff up. It was exciting and fun."

"I'd always felt that a vampire was as spooky as we could get," says Curtis. "That if the viewers bought it, we could get away with anything. If it didn't work, I figured we could always drive a stake into his heart."

It worked, and Barnabas Collins was spared the stake. The big question at the beginning, though, was how would one go about introducing a vampire to the average viewer and find an actor capable of making the character a believable one? This was the problem facing Curtis and company, and it was an original one at that. They needed an actor who could play a member of the undead naturally and yet pass himself off as a human being. Plans called for said thespian to create havoc for a short time until the ratings went up to a respectable level, and then the vampire would be dispatched.

"At the time," smiles Costello, "we had no idea that the vampire would be the element that saved us, and we were very cautious about approaching it."

As the vampire story drew ever closer, Curtis was in Europe and Costello was left in charge of casting the role.

"We were down to the wire," he says, "and still looking at actors. As a matter of fact, I had to pose for the portrait of Barnabas that hangs in Collinwood, except for the face, of course. Incidentally, I got the name Barnabas off a tombstone in Flushing, Queens. I don't remember the last name, but it was registered in Flushing and dated back to, I think, the eighteenth century. The name just sounded right."

During casting calls, an indifferent actor named Jonathan Frid arrived at the studio. Truth be told, Frid couldn't be bothered. Getting tied to a soap opera was contrary to his plans of going to California and becoming an instructor of drama, and he had come to the studio only to placate his agent. "At the time," Frid recalls, "I said, 'Swell, I'm never going to get it, so why am I wasting my time?' I think that because I was in that frame of mind, I ended up getting the job."

Director John Sedwick offers, "We felt Jonathan played it very honestly. He had a wonderful, mysterious sort of quality . . . a larger than life quality. He could be an English gentleman, on one hand, and, on the other, he could look evil and exude this vampire-undead mystique."

"When Jonathan Frid appeared," interjects Costello, "we said, 'That's it.' He couldn't have been costumed any faster. A couple of days later, he was in the coffin."

The rest, clichés be damned, was history.

"Barnabas was brought in because I wanted to see exactly how much I could get away with," relates Curtis, "never intending that he would be anything more than a vampire that I would drive a stake into. I wanted to see how far I could go on the show into the supernatural, and I figured there was nothing more bizarre than a vampire."

Frid, too, believed the engagement would not last long, especially after he shot his first episode. "I was so bloody nervous," he admits. "I was absolutely terrified because of the amount of money involved with a television show. That scared me. I just knew I'd be canned over the weekend. I was waiting for the phone call. I was shocked that they allowed me to come back. What happened was that the fear and discomfort registered in the performance. When I saw myself on the air, my eyes were so glazed over with terror that I scared myself. It was fear and nervousness that gave me my style."

Dark Shadows was on its way to becoming a cult hit and a pop-culture phenomenon. Curtis had a new star. "Who knew?" the producer asks. "I brought the vampire in and it suddenly became this gigantic hit. Then I thought, 'Now what am I going to do?' I couldn't kill him off, so that's when I turned him into the reluctant vampire. It really caught the imagination of the audience. *Dark Shadows* came from my mind as the way I remembered the classic horror films that were around when I was a kid, even though they weren't that way. That was my memory of them. It was the same haunting quality we were after."

Explains Ron Sproat, "Dan hated a lot of what we blocked out story-wise, because it made Barnabas sympathetic. Dan never wanted him to be sympathetic. We just felt we couldn't get that much mileage out of a character who is pure evil. It isn't interesting, anyway. When you're dealing with two and a half hours a week and you're seeing a lot of the character, it just has to have more dimension than that. Even the villain has to have different colors other than snarling and snapping. In fact, in the book *Dracula,* Dracula hardly appears at all. He's in the beginning and the end, but most of it's the search for him. Anyway, that's how that evolved. Our ratings started going up when the vampire came on."

The challenge of building this reluctant vampire characterization was tossed to Frid, who had studied at London's Royal Academy of Dramatic Arts and earned a master's in directing from the Yale School of Drama. "The irony is that I'm not a horror fan," muses Frid. "I remember seeing Bela Lugosi in *Dracula* when I was very young, but I graduated very quickly to Cary Grant pictures and had no more interest in horror."

Frid decided it would be best to approach an unrealistic role in a realistic manner. "I know I had a good approach to the character," he says. "I tried to make him a perfectly sensible person. I never played a vampire. I played him as a man with a hell of a conflict, but I never could perfect what I wanted to do, and that stiffness just fed Barnabas because he was so uptight."

In terms of explaining the appeal of Barnabas, Sproat offers, "I think part of it is because [Jonathan] played a duality, and had kind of a lost quality as well. He said originally, and I think he was right, 'Don't write the evil. I'll play that. I look that way.' That's what he said. He also said that he'd done *Richard III,* and he was astounded by the reviews at the time, because they said he was the most evil Richard on record. He told me, 'I was playing for sympathy.' So he suggested that we write *against* the evil and he would play against it, which would make it more interesting. That's what we did and I thought it worked."

And the viewers responded. Ratings rose and the show inspired a variety of merchandise tie-ins as well as two motion pictures, the first of which, 1970's *House of Dark Shadows,* was released while the soap was still on the air.

With the success of Barnabas, Curtis opened the supernatural gates with a vengeance. He and Robert Costello introduced a warlock and a man-made monster, as well as a host of witches, werewolves, and ghosts. Lightning struck again when David Selby joined the cast as the silent spirit of Quentin Collins.

Ultimately, though, *Dark Shadows,* like most fads, began to run out of steam. Toward the end of its run, Curtis and the writing staff were reworking everything from *Dorian Gray* to *Dr. Jekyll and Mr. Hyde.* "I wanted to say goodbye to it so bad I couldn't see straight," admits Curtis. "We got around to the last year and I was completely tapped out idea-wise. And we ended up with some dreadful stories during the last year. It was like being in jail. At the end, I was barely associating with it anymore. I was so glad when they finally put me out of my misery and got me the hell out of there. I couldn't have gone on any longer."

Sam Hall most definitely has a theory as to why *Dark Shadows* ultimately ran out of creative steam as well as ratings.

"Dan was so insane," he states matter of factly. "He had never watched a soap opera, so after a year of success he began to say, 'We've got to get more scares, more romance, more mystery,' and finally ended up with plots . . . we had one plot I didn't even understand. Quentin had Petofi's mind, so Quentin spoke what Petofi would have said and Petofi spoke what Quentin would have said, and you needed subtitles. You had no idea what was happening. He'd say, 'This is what we're going to do,' and he'd get all charged up and run around the office with his golf clubs, putting shots into those little holes. We all said, 'Dan, you're crazy. No one's going to have the faintest idea what's going on.' 'No, no, it's right. Do it. Don't argue with me, do it.' So it was that kind of operation and every plot got stranger and stranger, and we just out-stranged ourselves. He really was convinced that the American audience had the short attention span that he himself had, which is not necessarily true."

Elaborating on this premise, Ron Sproat adds, "The show did change tone violently. At one point there were many disagreements about how it should be handled. I thought it was going too campy. I thought it got kind of crazy at the point where you have a witch who has been transformed into a vampire, talking to a man-made man who wants a man-made woman, and the Devil is walking around telling everybody what to do. Then there was another vampire, plus there was a werewolf. I was throwing my hands up in despair. Looking back on it, I thought there were other ways to handle it than the ways that were taken. There was a basic disagreement. I felt that it shouldn't be so fantastic, that there should be some root in reality; some sort of bizarre reality. Another writer felt it should be total fantasy, total craziness.

"Not only did we have indexes of stories," adds Sproat, "but Dan insisted that we had to have something happen at the end of every act. There had to be some sort of horrific suspense to get you through the next act. As a result of that, things happened that were terrible. They bumped off a major character, Sam Evans, at the end of Act Two and his daughter barely had time to say, 'My poor father died.' There came a point where no one knew what the hell was going on. We had arguments about that. I told Dan that I felt we owed a certain obligation to the person who isn't able to get to the television every day, to explain what's going on. That we should keep a fairly clear storyline. Fans didn't want to have a guide that would untangle all this."

Ultimately, they didn't need one. It all came to an end after 1,225 episodes on April 2, 1971. Yet the fans wouldn't let go. In the early eighties, *Dark Shadows* became the first daytime soap opera to go into syndicated reruns. Then, MPI Home Video issued every single episode on video cassettes and in January 1991 NBC announced they were reviving the show in a prime-time format, which was, in the end, short-lived.

When recrafting the show for NBC, Curtis says he didn't study the old *Dark Shadows,* but he still watches it for fun.

"It's still amazingly effective," he observes. "It looks crude by today's standards. We were working with a ridiculous little set. There are lots of mistakes—things falling down, people forgetting their lines. But, after all this time, you can still see what sucked in the audience. The magic is there."

JONATHAN FRID: *DARK SHADOWS*'S BARNABAS COLLINS, TAKE ONE

Andy Warhol said that someday, everyone will be famous for 15 minutes. While this may be an exaggeration of sorts, it is true that the public occasionally latches onto an individual, raising him or her to a fad level or, in some cases, to cult status.

In such situations, said cult objects touch a chord with the public in an unexplainable way and, in a whirlwind of hysteria, become a veritable phenomenon without even realizing it. They just wake up one day within its midst. Such was precisely the case with actor Jonathan Frid and his portrayal of Barnabas Collins on *Dark Shadows.*

"The success of that show and my character still surprises me to this day," says Frid.

Several things should be said about Jonathan Frid at the outset, primary among them being that he is not as one would expect.

Knowing him as Barnabas, it's almost (but not quite) disappointing to have him greet you at the door without a flowing black cape draped over his shoulders, candles in hand, and fangs protruding from his mouth.

His voice is gentler than one would expect from the world's second most renowned vampire, and while he is a bit grayer than he was on the series, his facial features remain virtually the same. His eyes, in particular, have the same vibrant quality they did all those years ago.

His apartment, as well, is not as one would expect. Rather than being a shrine to *Dark Shadows,* it is pleasantly decorated, with one wall devoted to a career that has encompassed everything from Shakespeare and T. S. Elliot to Barnabas Collins.

Jonathan is jovial and an easy talker. Yet as he speaks, one detects a certain amount of self-censorship, a protective device to shield his privacy as much as possible—a privacy that was unexpectedly swept out from beneath him in 1967.

"You must realize that being a star is as difficult an art as acting," he says earnestly. "You have to have the right people around you and you have to tell the right lies. You have to be Mr. Perfect from the moment you get up until the time you go to bed. I had a difficult time coping with all that . . . of dealing with this sudden lack of a private life."

This seems an ironic statement from an actor who had strived much of his life for the type of success that he suddenly found himself in.

The beginning of his attraction to the acting world can probably be traced to his childhood in Hamilton, Ontario, where, in prep school, the 15-year-old Frid made his debut as the "old" Sir Anthony Absolute in Sheridan's *The Rivals.*

"Of course, the most important role in my life was the first one," he says. "It was during *The Rivals* that I thought, 'Yes, acting is what I can do.' However, it wasn't until five years later, in 1945, while in the navy that it occurred to me to become a professional."

The actor explains that when a navy friend announced that he was "definitely" coming to New York after the war to become a professional, it gave him the same incentive.

Upon leaving the Canadian Navy, he went to England to study at the Royal Academy, which he quit after several terms because, "I wanted to get out and work," he says. "I found that many Canadian actors were making a lot of money playing Americans—and I'd gone to the Royal Academy for classical training."

He appeared in a successful film called *The Third Man,* portraying an American gangster, and returned to Canada in 1950 to play Dr. Sloper in *The Heiress.* Following this role, Frid studied at Toronto's Academy of Radio Arts under Lorne Green and then enrolled at Yale Drama School, where, in 1957, he received a master's degree in Fine Arts.

He moved to New York in 1957 and appeared in *The Golem,* Wallace Hamilton's *The Burning, Romeo & Juliet, Macbeth,* and *Richard III,* among others. Despite all this, however, the success he dreamed of seemed intangible.

Fate quite literally intervened in the beginning of 1967 and altered Frid's life in ways that even he could not foresee.

He had just wrapped up a national tour with Ray Milland in *Hostile Witness* and he planned to pack up his belongings from his apartment, move to California, and use his master's degree to get a job as a professor of drama.

"As I got to my apartment door in New York, the phone was ringing," he recalls. "I left my bags in the hall and ran in to answer it. It was my agent, whom I hadn't told when I'd be back. He told me about the part of a vampire on *Dark Shadows,* and coaxed me into trying out for it by pointing out that the job would only last a few weeks and would net me some extra money to go to the Coast with. Well, you know the rest of the story. It was just that freaky phone call. If I had been two minutes later . . ." His voice trails off, letting the silence speak for itself.

He joined the series in April of 1967. The ratings took off and fan mail began pouring in, including erotic letters and nude photos of women who wanted him to use his fangs on them. Vampire Barnabas Collins and Jonathan Frid were suddenly cult objects. But wasn't such a role rather bizarre for a classically trained actor?

"Actually, I think Barnabas is very much like everything I've played before," he differs. "I played Macbeth once, and there's a great similarity between Macbeth and Barnabas. Certainly, Macbeth is built on guilt, just as Barnabas was. It's a characteristic which even Richard III has, though I don't really like to drag Richard into it. A lot of people think that he had no guilt, and I think that he did." To illustrate this, he points out the nightmare sequence of Shakespeare's play in which Richard confronts the souls of his victims, and, consequently, himself.

"I've often portrayed the heavy and it's a type of role I enjoy playing," he relates. "My greatest 'heavy' role, next to Barnabas, I suppose, was definitely Richard III. It's the one which I would love to play again, though I'm almost getting too old for it." He pauses at this, his eyes taking on a contemplative look. "Richard III is a delightful role that can be played very comically, but I was playing it for horror."

With this, Frid gives an oration on the aspects of his portrayal that have apparently influenced many of his other roles.

"I love to play horror for horror's sake," he explains. "Inner horror . . . I never thought I created fear with the fang business of Barnabas. I always felt foolish doing that part of it. The horror part I liked was 'the lie.'

"There's nothing more horrible than looking someone in the eyes who's telling you a lie and you know it. Somehow that scares me more than anything else. Of course, I've never been physically attacked by anybody with a knife or a gun . . . or teeth, and that may be quite horrible. But in terms of the theater, I liked the inner drama rather than the outward manifestation. An inner conflict or emotional confrontation is more of a drama to me. That's why with Barnabas there were many scenes I was thrilled to do and why the show came alive so many times for me."

It was Barnabas's lie, his pretending to be something that he wasn't, that motivated Frid more than any other aspect of the role. "That pretense was something the actor playing Barnabas had to remember all the time," he emphasizes. "He got the lust for blood every once in a while, but always what preyed on his mind was the lie.

"And, of course, it played right into my lie as an actor," he adds. "I was lying that I was calm and comfortable in the studio, just as Barnabas was lying that he was the calm, comfortable cousin from England. He wasn't at all. He was a sick, unbelievable creep that the world didn't know about."

In essence, the character's facade inspired the actor, but what was it about Barnabas that appealed to so many people?

"First of all," he begins, obviously still trying to figure the whole thing out, "Barnabas was [a] sympathetic vampire. He was a man with an addiction who drank blood only to survive. The audience felt pity for him, and many of the women wanted to mother him. Secondly, I've always felt that there was a love/hate relationship between the audience—particularly children—and Barnabas. In some ways, he was looked upon as a darker version of Santa Claus; friendly enough that you were intrigued by him, yet mysterious enough that he frightened you."

And what about the overall appeal of *Dark Shadows* itself?

"I recently watched a re-run of an episode which I thought was excellent, and it gave me a perspective which is good for me to have. It took me out of my own ego trip in my connection to the show, because I wasn't even on it, and I think it answers that particular question.

"Grayson Hall as Dr. Hoffman and Robert Gerringer as Dr. Woodard were having an awful confrontation about me," he says. "This day, they were both dead on perfect and their confrontation sparked. It reinforced our interest in her getting her goals. Grayson was strong without overacting and made everything believable in this ridiculous story. But that's the magic of theater, making implausible things plausible. The writers scored that day as did the actors, and it was all very believable."

He continues, obviously enthused about this revelation regarding the show. "A great deal of the time the show was absolutely absurd, because we weren't strong enough to make it believable and we had an extra duty over and beyond the average soap opera. To deal with this strange material on a daily basis is more demanding on the actors than normal, and on the writers. Because of its inconsistency as a good and bad show, some days people would laugh at it as a hoot and then on others they would get caught up in it.

"I suppose what I'm really trying to say is that when the oversizeness is honestly thought out and meaningful, the show became sheer magic and I think it's as good as anything I've ever seen on television."

APPENDIX A: THE <u>DARK SHADOWS</u> CONNECTION

By the summer of 1967, it had become obvious that *Dark Shadows* was something of a sensation. Teenagers would gather outside the studio to get a glimpse of their favorite star, the fan mail had increased tenfold, and, thanks to a *New York Times* article that revealed that Frid had a listed phone number, fans would call at all hours of the night. It wasn't long before his likeness adorned lunch boxes, bubble gum cards, comic books, and more than two dozen paperback novels. One must assume that being thrust into this phenomenon was not an easy thing to deal with.

"Well, the cameras scared me because I hadn't had much experience in television," Frid admits. "Not so much the cameras, but the millions of dollars they represented. I was in big business and my job was to get people to hang in there until the next set of commercials. I was scared by that.

"The other aspect," he continues, "is the stardom. I guess I kind of realized what was happening after two or three months, but I was saved from dwelling on it and becoming too big for my boots because I was so busy with the scripts every day."

Actually, this does not seem so improbable when one understands Frid's approach to studying a script.

"The character of Barnabas was all set before we even began. My only problem was getting it under my belt. Getting the lines down, delivering them, and playing the values I had to play, the motivations. I spend so much time working out the problems that I don't get down to the nitty gritty and get the bloody lines learned. I'm constantly undoing whatever it is I'm doing. Tearing it apart so it's in a shambles, little pieces of paper all over the place. Then I have to be in front of the camera in half an hour, and I've got my part all over the place. I used to do this night after night after night. It's just in my nature."

Dark Shadows, according to Frid, began to lose some ground in the ratings war in 1968, and it was the arrival of David Selby as Quentin Collins—a character whose popularity rivaled that of Barnabas's—that kept the soap going.

"Actually what happened with David is that I went up to Dan Curtis when they were exploiting me in '68 (I was on five days a week) and said, 'Dan, you're overworking me. I think you should create another character and give me a run for my money.' He said, 'You don't want that,' and I said, 'I'd rather have anything than work these hours. Give me some competition.' They tried two or three things until Selby came along. The ratings were going down at that point, and we were delighted that Selby boosted them. I guess I was a little envious, but not much. If you let that prey on you, you're through. It lessened the load on me. I think if it hadn't been for Selby, the show would have gone off the air in four months. He gave it a much needed shot in the arm and it ran for another year and a half or so."

Success followed success, as Frid toured different cities on weekends, visited the White House, hosted pageants, appeared on TV talk shows, and starred in the big-budgeted motion picture *House of Dark Shadows,* which is *not* a film he's fond of.

"I was not happy with it," he admits candidly. "I thought the script was merely a rehash of the early episodes and it got too realistic. The show was more Brigadoonish and charmingly naïve. Collinsport was in Maine, but that was as close as you ever got to a specific geology. Once in a while somebody would mention Boston, but that's about it. The movie was constantly referring to New York, Boston, and other places. The movie had too much zipping, zapping, and too much silly violence for violence's sake. I don't know how many vampires ended up in that thing. The attitude was kind of like, first, I beat the shit out of Willie, and then we have to have a car crash.

"Anyway, I thought it was dull and lacked the charm of the soap opera. I did, however, think it was interesting to do, because I hadn't done a movie before and found that my lines in the film amounted to one episode in length, and were spread out over a period of five weeks. It shows how much soap opera people are taxed. We did the whole movie in five weeks, which made a lot of people nervous. To me, it was a luxury."

After a five-year run, the ratings declined and the show was canceled in April of 1971.

"The end wasn't really a great shock, because the writing on the wall was always there for me," he says. "Every time the show went up another notch, I figured it was peaking and that it would start to go down. It lasted a hell of a lot longer than I thought it would. It wasn't the average soap opera and they went through all the stories three or four times. We started repeating ourselves and the show burned out."

So, despite the adulation of hardcore fans, *Dark Shadows* faded into the corridors of time, and the hysteria that had snared Frid suddenly set him free again.

"I knew I couldn't make a career out of being a star, because I would have had to make a commitment to the occult," he states. "I have no interest in the occult at all. If I did make a career of it, I would have had to become an honorary member of every occult society in the country and get into vampirism. I just couldn't bear the thought of doing that. Look at Bela Lugosi, the poor man. He died and had himself buried in his Dracula cape. I never wanted to get like that."

Moving out of the shadows, Frid appeared live in *Murder at the Cathedral* and on film in Oliver Stone's *Seizure* and ABC's *The Devil's Daughter,* before dropping out of the public spotlight. Was the problem typecasting?

"I knew that was going to happen," he explains. "Actually, there was nothing to typcast except the fangs. As far as Barnabas was concerned, he was more of a full-blown character than anybody on the show. Frankly, if I had worked harder, I could have manipulated it or, indeed, exploited it. You see, being a star is a big job and you can never go back. You can try, but you always end up trying to top yourself."

Another thing that made him keep a low profile was a desire for a state of normalcy in his life again. For this reason, he had disassociated himself from continued interest in the show for nearly a decade.

"It was just such a pleasure to have my private life again," he says with a breath of relief. "I was just so bored with the whole *Dark Shadows* thing."

In fact, it wasn't until the early 1980s that Frid appeared at his first convention, and his interest has been resparked, at least to a certain degree.

"I think it's absolutely wonderful that the fans have kept this whole thing alive," he laughs. "And in a way, my reassociation with them has allowed me to utilize *Dark Shadows* as a springboard for a live show I've created."

This one-man show, which has gone through a variety of titles including *Genesis of Evil* and *Fools and Fiends*, has met with great success as the actor has taken it around the country.

"It's shaping up nicely," enthuses Frid, who co-starred in a recent revival of *Arsenic and Old Lace.* "I've had my vacation from show business and now it's time to get back to brass tacks."

The future bodes well, and Jonathan Frid, classical actor and consummate vampire, embraces it willingly.

BEN CROSS: *DARK SHADOWS*'S BARNABAS COLLINS, TAKE TWO

Amazing as it may seem, the old ABC daytime soap opera *Dark Shadows* is, at the time of this writing, celebrating its thirty-second anniversary. The series originally ran from 1966 to 1971, and its cult following continues to this day.

For a number of years, the show's fans clamored for a reunion of the original cast in either a new series or a feature film, much as was the case with *Star Trek.* After all, the leap to the big screen had already been done in the form of 1970's *House of Dark Shadows* and 1971's *Night of Dark Shadows.* But as the years passed and the original cast grew older, the idea of a reunion seemed less likely. Then, in 1990, former NBC president Brandon Tartikoff made the somewhat surprising announcement that *Dark Shadows* would indeed be returning to television but as a prime-time series featuring an all new cast. Images of *Star Trek: The Next Generation* came to mind, and, undoubtedly, the network hoped for a similar kind of success.

Unfortunately, the short-lived series, which debuted as a midseason replacement show but suffered ratings challenges from the Gulf War, chose to merely remake the original storylines, which had already been remade in the aforementioned *House of Dark Shadows.* In fact, for the four-hour miniseries premiere, producer/director Dan Curtis chose to use many of the exact same camera set-ups and lines of dialogue that he had used in that film. Audiences didn't take to the new series, and it was swiftly canceled.

In its brief tenure, though, *Dark Shadows* cast the highly acclaimed actor Ben Cross, best known for his work in *Chariots of Fire,* as the new Barnabas Collins, taking over the role made famous by Jonathan Frid.

Like his predecessor, Cross chose to characterize Barnabas as a reluctant vampire, with a level of sensuality that played right into the hands of women susceptible to such things. Like many vampires, Barnabas remains extremely attractive to the female sex.

"I have no idea [why]," Cross admits. "I can make certain—certain, dare I say, intelligent guesses as to why. I think one of the first things is the way women might view a vampire and vampire tale is somewhat different to the way a man would. We learn in the series—I mean, the series gets to a certain point where we simply have to go back to the past and find out exactly what went on. And so we do go back. We see Barnabas as this really very, very nice guy. Very, very happy family. And it's really like a cautionary tale for married men. He actually has a fling with the wrong person. And the phrase of hell having no fury like a woman scorned, is absolutely true, because, in fact, she comes from Hell. And so, in a sense, he makes a human mistake that a lot of people, if they're honest, have actually made. He regrets it, and then becomes a victim and a vampire. So, in a sense, he is as much a victim of his own condition, in the way that the people he finds himself biting."

Cross had previously played a vampire in a USA Cable film, *Night Life,* and one has to wonder if the English-born actor is fearful of being typecast.

"I've played three Jews in my life," he differs. "I've played four priests; I've played various Middle Eastern gentlemen. I don't think I'm in any danger of being typecast per se, because I've played two vampires. They were totally different. So I'm really not worried. Of course, I [did] have to worry in the back of my mind, that if the series [was] as successful as everybody [hoped], that after five years I [would] be indelibly identified with this character. But, for instance, I do have a rather brighter shadow that's followed me for ten years, which is a film I made. And it really hasn't done me a lot of harm. On the contrary, from my point of view I'm trying to make the character as complex and as interesting and as fascinating as I can on every single level. Except Dan Curtis insists that he doesn't have a sense of humor, or if he does he doesn't show it."

Despite Curtis's objections, Cross relishes that a certain level of humor did pervade the series. For instance, in the miniseries Barnabas described his career as being all-consuming.

"There are quite a few moments like that," he smiles. "Dare I say some I put in myself. Some are in the script, like that one, and some I put in myself. There's one thing to be aware of a situation being funny, and it's another thing for my character to actually crack into a smile or laugh. So there is a fine line there. I also have to be very careful. I don't want him to be flippant—I'm sure you'll understand what I mean when I say the James Bond sense. That's punning on a situation which is kind of cute. There's nothing cute about Barnabas, and I wouldn't play him cute. There is an area there where he can show not so much a humorous [and] comedic side, but just a softer, more aware of the kind of farcical aspect of his situation."

Admittedly, the announcement that Cross would be starring in the series was somewhat surprising to people.

"Let me answer you in a roundabout way," he says. "I certainly wouldn't have done it five years ago, for reasons that aren't particularly interesting in this situation. But there comes a point when what you would not have done in the past, becomes feasible for one reason or another now, and may not be so in the future. The most important thing is that although I've worked here in the States, and I've certainly worked for many American companies, I never really had the experience of working full-time in the American television industry. It was an experience up to that point that had been denied me for one reason or another. And I really thought it was actually about time I committed myself to the American television system to find out what it was all about. And hopefully with a project that I found interesting and fun.

"Really, I had to make decisions about what I didn't like about this kind of project. And I'm more satisfied about myself, about things that I once viewed as negatives. For instance, [I was asked if] each week kind of completes a story within itself that has a beginning, a middle, and an end, i.e., *Moonlighting* or something like that. The answer is no. And I was not going to be interested in any way, shape, or form in that kind of series about a vampire. I feel that there were much more interesting areas. It's more like a psychological study, an exploration of the whole mythology of vampirism.

"And," Cross notes, "when I was satisfied that it was going in that particular direction, it was fairly easy for me because it's an extraordinary story and an extraordinary character. And I can promise you I'm not exaggerating when I say it's really one of the most challenging roles I've ever played, because I have to come up with something new every episode."

A LONG LINE OF VAMPIRES AND VAMPIRE SLAYERS

BELA LUGOSI: THE ORIGINAL DRACULA

In the 1930s, Bela Lugosi captured the world's imagination as Bram Stoker's Count Dracula, a role that would ultimately take over the actor's life . . . and death.

"Every actor's greatest ambition is to create his own definitive and original role," he said in 1934. "A character with which he will always be identified. In my case, that role was Dracula."

He was born in 1882 as Bela Balasko in the Hungarian town of Lugo, Lugosi. He grew up to become a blacksmith but ultimately decided to follow acting, performing on stage in Hungary. He came to New York in 1921 and managed to score roles in a variety of silent films, usually as a bad guy. As he noted to one journalist, "I find that, because of my language and gestures, that I am catalogued as what you call a heavy. My accent stamped me, in the imagination of the producers, as an enemy. Therefore, I must be a heavy."

When a stage production of *Dracula* that had failed in London was given a shot in the United States in 1927, Lugosi was offered the role. "Somebody connected with the play had seen one of my films and mentioned me to the producer and director of *Dracula*," said Lugosi. "They came and saw me in the play *Open House* and believed I was the only actor in America suitable for the part and wanted me to audition. It was a complete change from the kind of characters I was playing."

Lugosi performed the role on stage in New York, Los Angeles, and back in England, where he turned the show into something of a hit. Unfortunately, he could not continue performing the show. "The role seemed to demand that I keep myself worked up to a fever pitch," he related to journalists. "And so I sat in my dressing room and, as nearly as possible, I took on the actual attributes of Dracula. I was laboring under a great strain. When I came off stage after a scene, I went straight to my dressing room and did not emerge until it was time for me to go on again. I was under a veritable spell that I dared not break. If I stepped out of my character for even a moment, the seething menace of the terrible Count Dracula would be gone."

In 1930, he essayed the role for Universal's film adaptation of Stoker's story. "In playing Dracula in the picture," he told *Hollywood Filmograph Magazine,* "I found that there was a great deal that I had to unlearn. In the theater I found that I was not only playing to the spectators in the front row but also to those in the last row of the gallery. Because of that, there was a lot of exaggeration in everything I did. But, for the screen, I found that a great deal of repression was absolutely necessary. [Director] Tod Browning has had to continually hold me down. In my other screen roles I did not have this difficulty. But I have played Dracula a thousand times on stage and have become thoroughly settled into the technique of the stage. But thanks to director Browning, I am unlearning fast."

Universal's *Dracula* was a tremendous success, and Lugosi immediately found himself desperately trying to break free of the confines of the genre, going so far as to turn down the role of the monster in the studio's adaptation of *Frankenstein.* Unfortunately, the actor's desperation was such that he agreed to star in just about every film that came his way, among them (between 1931 and 1934) *Murders in the Rue Morgue, Broad Minded, White Zombie,* and *Chandu the Magician.* In 1935 he reteamed with Browning on *Mark of the Vampire,* which was praised for its atmospheric filming. Four years later he portrayed Igor in *Son of Frankenstein.*

In the mid-thirties he gave an interview, in which he detailed, "A strange thing happened to me following *Dracula*. I discovered that every producer in Hollywood had set me down as a type, an actor for this kind of role. Considering that before Dracula I had never played anything but leads and straight characters, I was both amused and disappointed at what was happening. In the case of Dracula, I found this [stereotyping] to be almost fatal. It took me years to live down Dracula and to convince film producers that I could play almost any other type of role."

In 1941 he gave a nice turn as a Gypsy in *The Wolfman* but then ended up in less successful films, among them *Return of the Vampire*, *The Body Snatchers*, *The Ape Man*, *Voodoo Man*, *Return of the Ape Man*, and *Scared to Death*. Another turn as Dracula followed in 1948's *Abbott & Costello Meet Frankenstein*, in which he managed to be extremely credible despite the shenanigans going on around him. Even with that highlight in his career, things continued to get worse in the fifties, with such efforts as *Mother Riley Meets the Vampire*, *Bela Lugosi Meets a Brooklyn Gorilla*, *Bride of the Monster*, *Glen or Glenda*, and, in his last role, the so-called worst movie of all time, *Plan Nine from Outer Space*.

Before his death—accelerated by alcohol and drug abuse—in 1956, he mused to journalists, "I look in the mirror and I say to myself, 'Can it be that you once played Romeo?' Always, it is the same. When a film company is in the red, they come to me and say, 'Okay, so we make a horror film.' And so that is what we do. It is what I always do."

CHRISTOPHER LEE: STAKING A CLAIM AS DRACULA

In many ways, Christopher Lee's Dracula was the antithesis of Lugosi's. Whereas his predecessor had provided menace with subtlety and spoke in very measured tones, Lee's interpretation of the character—beginning with 1958's *Horror of Dracula*—was more of a snarling creature who let his fangs do the talking for him.

"I see Dracula first and foremost as a nobleman of great dignity, power, presence, and physical impact," he said during the production of 1965's *Dracula, Prince of Darkness.* "He is a man of brooding stillness. I see him as an inhuman entity who is controlled by a force that is beyond his powers of control." Elsewhere, he said, "The first Dracula *[Horror of Dracula]* was a very good picture. In a way, it's a classic and the reason is very easy to see. It was the nearest to Stoker's book and it was transferred to the screen with a certain fidelity to the author's intention."

As for *Horror of Dracula,* he related, "I tried to remain true to the book. What came onto the screen was a combination of my having read the book and trying to invest the character with dignity, nobility, ferocity, and sadness. I decided that my source would be Bram Stoker's novel. It was about a vampire not at all like me in physical character, but there were aspects of him with which I could readily identify—his extraordinary stillness, punctuated by bouts of manic energy with feats of strength belying his appearance; his power complex; the quality of being done for but undead; and by no means least the fact that he was an embarrassing member of a great and noble family."

Lee's Dracula series, produced by England's Hammer Studios, continued with *Dracula Has Risen from the Grave* (1968), *Taste the Blood of Dracula* (1969), and *Scars of Dracula* (1970), and the series rapidly fell into a formula. "I've become very much disenchanted with the way the character is presented in the films," Lee related in 1972. "I hope, when people see me playing this character, that they realize that I am struggling against insufferable odds on occasion to remain faithful to the author's original character. *Scars of Dracula* was truly feeble. It was a story with Dracula popped in. Even the Hammer makeup for once was tepid. It's one thing to look like death warmed up, quite another to look unhealthy. I was a pantomime figure. Everything was over the top, especially the giant bat whose electrically motored wings flapped with slow deliberation as if it were doing morning exercises. The idea that Dracula best liked his blood served in a nubile container was gaining ground with the front office, and I struggled in vain against the direction that the fangs should be seen to strike home, as against the more decorous (and more chilling) methods of shielding the sight with the Count's cloak."

Lee went back to basics in the Spanish film *El Conde Dracula,* in which he finally got to portray Dracula the way that Stoker had written him. From there, he segued back to the Hammer films with *Dracula A.D. 1972,* which took place in modern-day London. "I think it's all wrong," Lee said in *The Dracula Book.* "I think it's totally and completely wrong to take it out of context and out of the historical, Gothic period and to put it in modern times. But, in a weird sort of way, it quite works. I was aghast at the plan to bring the story into modern times, but a compromise was effected whereby at least his Gothic homestead and the church were retained. . . . [But] the hippie idiom used was already out of date when the film was made and the programme at large felt wrong to me. That was just about bearable, with strong misgivings." An even lower mark was reached in the final Hammer Dracula film, *The Satanic Rites of Dracula,* in which Dracula and a mad scientist plot the conquest of the world. Said Lee, "With *Satanic Rites,* I reached my irrevocable full stop. Thereafter I flung myself out in the snow for the wolves to gorge themselves on, leaving the thing to carry on without me."

While Lee—who had become Dracula for an entire generation—had struggled to maintain the quality of the series, his view in retrospect was a bit more forgiving than it had been during the actual production of the series. "Looking back at them," he said in 1981, "I find that there is nothing in the Dracula movies that I've done that I'm ashamed of. Some of the Dracula films were better than others, but I obviously enjoyed doing them or I would not have kept going back to them. At this point, I would have to say that I'm not completely finished with Dracula. If someone came along with a really good script that showed the character the respect it deserved, then, of course, I would play Dracula again."

BARRY ATWATER: THE NIGHT STALKER

The late Barry Atwater can be recognized on a wide variety of television series and motion pictures, including *Nightmare, The Wrong Man, The Twilight Zone, Star Trek,* and *Kung Fu.* To horror fans, it is undoubtedly his portrayal of vampire Janos Skorzeny in the TV movie *The Night Stalker* that leaves the greatest impression.

The Night Stalker, of course, introduced audiences to reporter Carl Kolchak, whose investigation of a string of murders leads him to the lair of a real-life vampire residing in Las Vegas. In Atwater's more than capable hands, Skorzeny became a true creature of the night as the actor conveyed myriad emotions without uttering a single word.

"I felt [Skorzeny] was very lonely," Atwater explained in the 1970s. "He has no friends. He's all alone, so he doesn't talk to people. I'm sure he's not a happy man, but he's stuck. I just figured here's a guy who *needs* blood. I figured he can't be very different from a guy who needs heroin, who's an addict. I've never taken heroin and never intend to, but what I heard about it is that a guy has to have it. If Skorzeny didn't have blood, what would happen to him? It must be really hell not to have blood.

"It's not a question of being immoral or cruel," he added. "It's a question of 'I've got to have it!' Do it, that's all. 'It's too bad if people die, I'm sorry about that, but I have this hang-up. I don't want to kill anyone. I don't get kicks by killing people. I simply have to have it.' And if people don't understand it, it's not my fault—and they chase me and they do awful things to me and they shoot bullets and I'm furious with them. The people who were chasing me were my enemies. *They* were the 'heavies,' the 'villains.'"

Atwater was chosen by producer Dan *(Dark Shadows)* Curtis to portray Janos Skorzeny, based on a series of photographs. The actor, upon reading the Richard Matheson teleplay that was based on an unpublished Jeff Rice novel, was hooked.

"I really didn't have to study [the script] because I had no lines," Atwater detailed. "But I began to think about the part, what I'd do with it. This is almost automatic—when you pick up a script, your mind begins to work, you don't have to tell it to. I was very glad [I didn't have lines], because I think as soon as the vampire opens his mouth and starts to talk, he becomes an ordinary human being; an actor saying silly lines. And I think that was a brilliant idea of theirs not to have the vampire say a word."

Overall, he was quite happy to have been involved with the film in the first place.

"The script was excellent," Atwater enthused, "a really tight script. Richard Matheson apparently has the ability to visualize in his mind's eye what he wants to see on the screen, and he writes curt directions. A good recipe. Our director, John Llewellyn Moxey, was able to capture good shots, and the cutter, Desmond Marquette, who I don't think has gotten nearly enough credit, put it together so that it moved at a very fast pace. There was no 'dead air' in that story."

ROBERT QUARRY:
COUNT YORGA RISES AGAIN

Actor Robert Quarry has a tenacity that would impress Count Yorga. How else would you explain a man getting struck by a drunk driver and, as a result, being unable to work for three years—then making a comeback?

"Three years out of this business is a long time, as strange as that may seem," the former vampire star notes without bitterness. Quarry's voice remains calm and even, whether he's talking about the tragic accident that halted his career and took the life of his dog, or discussing the problems of re-establishing himself in Hollywood. Yet despite everything, Quarry is back in action, having completed a variety of actioners, *Commando Squad, Cyclone,* and *The Phantom Empire,* among them.

"*Cyclone* is about some kind of strange motorcycle that shoots rockets and runs over neo-Nazis," Quarry explains with a laugh. "It's one of those movies with scores of chases, crashes, and fireballs leaping around. I'm supposed to be an undercover agent, but it turns out that I'm working for the other side, so I'm the villain—as usual. It's the regular heavy role, but at least it isn't too weird, although a movie about a motorcycle that can do just about anything has to be a little weird.

"I get blown up at the end, and I move on to the next movie. But that's my reputation, although I did have fun on this one. The filmmakers are all kids, so when I tell them that I'm old and can't get up at 4:00 AM, they say, 'Get this old man out here!'" Quarry laughs. "It was fun working again and feeling good. Most important of all, it convinced me that I could still do it, so now I'm looking for other projects.

"People remember me, and some of them rather fondly, from the *Count Yorga* films," he continues, "but because everything is so realistic these days, some casting folks think that you have to be weird to have played fantasy roles. When I first started doing the horror films, it was nice. I made a little money and a little reputation. But then, suddenly, every kid who wanted to make some horror film would send me these terrible scripts. And I never got asked to do anything else. These people would think of fangs and baying at the moon and call me. Enough time has probably gone by, however, and if I can meet with the younger casting agents who don't think I've beaten mother and thrown the baby in the middle of the freeway, I'll be okay."

Quarry began his career at age 14 when Alfred Hitchcock came to Santa Rosa to make his classic *Shadow of a Doubt*. The aspiring actor, who had loved films all his life, went down to the local hotel where the cast and crew would be staying and nabbed a job as a bellhop.

"I was such a dingbat," he recalls joyfully, "that the company took me under their wings, and Hitchcock wanted to get me a small contract at Universal. The only way they could do it was to have me play a little scene, so he gave me about two lines. They were cut, and right then I should have known that my career was not going to be easy. I was cut out of the first movie that I ever did, but at least it got me my contract."

The actor appeared briefly in a variety of films, then moved on to radio, summer stock, and eventually television, where he began playing "the heavy."

"That's how I got typecast. No matter what age I was," Quarry smiles. "I was a creep. I used to think that casting agents would write letters to each other saying, 'Robert Quarry: Mean Mother.' In actuality, I don't mind being the villain, because if you're not the leading man, there's nothing worse than being the second leading man. He's the one who says, 'My wife's in trouble, can you help?' I want to be the one who punches the wife out, only because it's interesting."

Staying in the system, Quarry appeared in such movies as *Agent for H.A.R.M.* and *WUSA* but didn't make a name for himself until he starred in the 1970 horror hit *Count Yorga: Vampire.* Easily his most popular and successful film, it cast him as the title vampire and was an effective thriller that has developed something of a cult following since its release nearly three decades ago. He was instantly established as the major new star of the genre, giving a performance that some said rivaled Christopher Lee's Dracula.

Amazingly, *Count Yorga* started as a skin flick. "Michael Macready and Bob Kelljan had made a soft-core porno film, kind of like those high school/college kid movies. With their initial investment of $14,000, they made about $60,000," recalls Quarry. "So Bob decided to write a soft porn vampire movie. We had been friends for a long time, and I called him up and said, 'Why the hell don't you do this in the horror genre? There's a big horror market, and you could then make some good bucks. And if you do it that way, I'll play Count Yorga.'

"So they did it. They kept a couple of sequences in it that would easily allow the film to become a soft-porn production if it didn't go over well as a horror film. But it turned out pretty well. AIP bought it and that's that. The whole picture was made for $64,000, and it made millions. It was shot very quickly and very economically. I got paid about $1,229. When I saw that they had made millions, it was the only time I ever got kind of snotty about anything. I thought, 'Hey, the film got incredible reviews and it does work because of me. There's no two ways about it.' That doesn't sound very humble, but it's true that my performance was a classic. So, I received a bonus check for $350. Isn't that grand?"

Nonetheless, Quarry remains quite pleased with his characterization of the undead Count Yorga.

"When I first read it," he comments, "I just thought it was campy crap. That's all it was. My approach was to incorporate some humor but make him real. Originally, they wanted to do it with a dialect, but there was no way I would be doing all of that crap. I was fighting against the Bela Lugosi image and Christopher Lee's Dracula. Not that there was anything wrong with either one of them, but they were unreal in a certain way and I wanted to give Yorga a kind of reality and play him straight. Then, I could jump out of the woodwork and bite everybody."

Like all great past vampires, Quarry had considerable "fang" difficulties. "You couldn't talk in them for one thing," details the actor. "I had a great line, which I was supposed to say with the fangs in. Then, I would go into the studio and dub it. It's the only line I can remember from any film I've done: 'Soon I will suck from your veins the sweet nectar of life, then we shall be as one in a lifetime of eternal bliss.' When I had my teeth in, it went like this: 'Thoon I will thuck from your veinth the thweet nectar of life, then we thall be ath one in a lifetime of eternal blith.' I sounded like Daffy Duck! We took it out, because it was such a ridiculous line, but Bob, who loved it, put it back into *The Return of Count Yorga*. I had to say that line to Mariette Hartley, and thirty-seven takes later we got it on film."

The box office success of *Count Yorga* also resulted in AIP's signing Quarry to a seven-year contract and their attempting to groom him as the next horror star. First up, naturally, was a sequel, the aforementioned *Return of Count Yorga*.

"Quite simply," explains Quarry, "AIP made a lot of money on the first one, so they wanted to do a sequel. That was going to be my first picture for them on the contract. It did very well, though not as well as the original. Then again, most sequels don't."

The vampire star followed *Return of Count Yorga* with *The Deathmaster* (a.k.a. *Khorda*), which, incredible as it may seem, cast him as a vampire guru.

"I wanted to make some producer's money on a film, so I had an idea to do a movie about a Charles Manson type of vampire," Quarry recalls. "This was right after the Manson thing, and the attitude was 'Let's jump on anything that's exploitable.' Manson took all of those kids and converted them into murderers. My story had them converted into vampires. I thought it would be a good plot. Then, I went off to England to do a play. My partner hired some writer to do the script and when I got back, it was the worst script ever written. I got a very good cameraman to shoot it, so at least it would look good, but the problem was that we didn't really have much of a script, and there was no time to do a rewrite. We tried to fix it up as we went along, but it was impossible.

"In fact," he chuckles, "when Elvira showed it on TV, she stopped the film in the middle and said, 'Gee, are they making this up as they go along?' I called her at the studio, laughing, and said that we *were* making it up as we went along. We had a good time shooting it, but *Deathmaster* was not exactly a masterpiece."

Next on his agenda was *Dr. Phibes Rises Again,* sequel to Vincent Price's quintessential revenge movie *The Abominable Dr. Phibes.* Quarry played Phibes's eternal life-seeking rival.

"It was tremendous fun working with Price," Quarry admits, "and it was a damn good movie. I was so pleased to be doing a film that cost more than $34. Add to that the fact that it was shot in London, my favorite city in the world, and you have a very enjoyable experience."

Unfortunately, a situation developed at AIP where the company just wanted to fulfill the contract with the actor as quickly as possible.

"Each movie started to get progressively worse," laments Quarry. "Like *Madhouse,* which was the last picture Vincent and I did together.

We arrived in England on Saturday, they sent the script to us Sunday night. We called each other and agreed that it was the worst piece of crap we had ever read. They were really just trying to get rid of us at that point. Vincent's contract was up and mine still had another year to go on it.

"The terrible thing," he adds with regret, "is that there were a couple of good TV things offered to me, but I couldn't do horror films on TV or movies as long as I was under contract to them. I could play villains, but the hot thing to do at that moment was to use the good publicity I was getting in the horror films. People wanted me for those things, but AIP said no. Meanwhile, they did not do anything about finding new properties that were very good."

While he had to turn down the title role in the great TV movie *The Night Stalker,* Quarry did join the cast of *Sugar Hill,* a blaxploitation voodoo potboiler.

"My contract was play or pay," he says. "Rather than pay me, they would play me and they ruined the whole movie as far as the producer and director were concerned. Actually, as it turned out, I was the best actor in it. I was the head of the black mafia in Houston. It was a weird movie, but that's the way I finished my contract at AIP, being starred in an all-black movie."

For a long time, *Sugar Hill* was Quarry's last major film, but things are changing now. While he manages to segue from film to film, there is talk regarding a new Count Yorga sequel.

"I'll have to lose thirty-five pounds. I quit smoking and a little Raymond Burr is trying to get out. I've always liked Yorga because when we started doing them, I brought in many ideas, including giving him a sense of humor. He was aware he was his own 'camp,' so he played that in public, besides being a monster on the side. I like him because I felt like he belonged to me, and it wouldn't bother me in the least to play the role again. Of course, I don't know if it would be any good, or if there's an audience for it anymore. Of all the horror things I've done, it was one of the more interesting characters I had to play.

"So why not a third film?" the 60-plus-year-old comeback kid asks rhetorically. "I'm interested in anything that's work these days. I'm so tired of the teenage movies where they're all just looking to get laid. If there are three *Porky's* films, why not do another *Count Yorga?* Hell, it would be clean, wholesome living compared to that crap."

FRANK LANGELLA: SENSUALIZING DRACULA

In the late 1970s, Broadway audiences were introduced to a very different kind of Count Dracula. Though he was deadly when he had to be, this incarnation of Bram Stoker's member of the undead was more romantically inclined with his victims, and drank their blood to survive, not out of a willing desire to cause harm.

"Dracula is not a ghoul," Langella explained at the time. "I decided to play him as a lonely, troubled monarch with a sense of humor and a unique social problem. I see him as a noble man with a quiet secret. Not a man who goes around attacking victims, but instead seduces them. He is *compelled* to drink the blood of innocent victims."

In researching the role, one thing Langella did not do was study prior interpretations of the character.

"I did not go back to look at the old Draculas," he said. "I felt that I had to find a way that would make him work today. I came up with an erotic and vulnerable man who is lonely and can fall in love. I never saw him as a guy dripping blood all the time."

During its Broadway run, it was obvious that Langella's take on the character was right on the mark, judging by nightly reactions from the audience.

"When I come to play the love scenes on stage," he smiled, "there is an audible swooning and sighing from the women in the audience."

The actor performed the character on stage for approximately a year. Within 24 hours of his last performance he found himself in England, shooting the cinematic adaptation of the play under the directorial guidance of John Badham. Although he was delighted with the chance to bring Dracula to the screen, he found the experience to be quite different than on the stage. "Basically," he explained, "I went in trying to hold on to the inner core of the character as best I could. Whether or not he's erotic is up to the audience. I went from a situation where I had total control of the character to almost none at all."

Those who have viewed the film are pretty much split down the middle in terms of whether or not it works. There's no denying that Langella is a powerful screen presence, and he is effortlessly able to exude the character's sensuality as well as invoke terror, a point driven home by the fact that his Dracula does not bare fangs at all, yet he is completely believable.

Recently issued on DVD, Badham's version of *Dracula* remains an under-appreciated classic in the genre and one deserving of rediscovery.

FRIGHT NIGHT

One of the most effective vampire movies ever made was *Fright Night,* in which teenager Charlie Brewster (William Ragsdale) realizes that his next-door neighbor, Jerry Dandridge (Chris Sarandon), is actually a vampire. Desperate, Charlie turns to famous movie vampire hunter

Peter Vincent (Roddy McDowall). This 1985 film was a sly mixture of chills and laughs, with then-unprecedented special effects for a film in this genre. What follows are profiles of writer/director Tom Holland and stars McDowell and Sarandon.

Tom Holland

Try as he might, writer/director Tom Holland seems unable to avoid the horror genre, despite warnings from his peers that it would be, if you'll pardon the expression, death to be trapped there.

After making his directorial debut on the highly successful *Fright Night,* Holland searched for something that would be completely different and found it in Whoopi Goldberg's *Fatal Beauty.* Unfortunately, the film was so poorly received, both critically and commercially, that it is not even listed among his credits. Moving back into more familiar territory, he next gave audiences *Child's Play,* which was a tremendous hit, re-establishing Holland and making Chucky a household name. Other credits include two forays into the world of Stephen King—ABC's *The Langoliers* miniseries and the feature film *Thinner.*

Beginning as an actor before seguing into the roles of screenwriter and director, Tom Holland has quite literally climbed the motion picture ladder of success, fulfilling a dream he's had since childhood.

"I've always been interested in film," Holland explains reverently. "When I was four or five, I was glued to the television, and I went to see every movie that I could. I don't think that I really cared about anything else."

His entry level in the business, as stated before, was as an actor; he appeared in more than 250 commercials, three soap operas *(Love of Life, Flame in the Wind,* and *A Time for Us),* and films such as *The Model Shop* and *A Walk in the Spring Rain.* Feeling creatively stifled, he turned his talents to writing.

"When I got in the business," says Holland, "I didn't know it would take so long to learn to write. I've worked my way through writing into directing. I was so naïve. I came out in the early seventies, and that was at the time when all these original screenplays were going for $250,000. Then those screenwriters would turn around and direct. There were a lot of guys around who seemed to be doing it, and I thought I'd sit down, whip off a screenplay for a quarter of a million dollars, then write another one and direct it. I had no idea how hard writing was. So, ten years later, after I had, to some degree, mastered the craft of story-telling in a screenplay, I finally felt I could go on and direct. It's been a very slow, but sane forward progression."

This progression resulted in the screenplays for *The Beast Within, The Class of 1984,* and *Scream for Help,* a Hitchcockian tale in which a young girl suspects that her stepfather plans to murder her mother but can't prove it. The latter led to what may be considered one of Holland's most prestigious scripts, *Psycho II.*

"From what I understand," recalls Holland, "Robert Bloch had done a novel called *Psycho II,* then came to Universal and suggested that they make it into a film. They didn't like his book, but they thought the idea of a sequel was a great one. Richard Franklin was chosen as director, and while he was reading material looking for a writer, he found *Scream for Help.* On that basis, he hired me. Then the question was, What the hell was the story going to be?"

The answer was soon evident. *Psycho II,* taking place 22 years after the original, begins with Norman Bates being set free from the mental institution and trying to get his life on track again. Unfortunately, Lila Loomis

(Vera Miles), sister of the slain Marion Crane (see the original), wants revenge and sets about driving Norman crazy again. Needless to say, it's only a short matter of time before she's successful, and Mother makes a return appearance.

"I was trying desperately to be respectful," Holland says. "I didn't want to do a slasher film, but at the same time, as you can tell from some parts of the film, there was a feeling from the studio that there should be enough shock moments to satisfy that 'slice and dice' crowd out there. Given today's market, I couldn't really disagree with them. It was also, if you think about it historically, the first *Psycho* that opened up the whole genre.

"I don't think anybody picked up a knife and graphically did somebody in until Hitchcock got Janet Leigh in the shower," he elaborates. "I think that sort of set everybody's mind working. They took it a lot farther, God knows. The serial murders, the nonstoryline murders, may have started with *Halloween* or *Friday the 13th,* but I don't think the graphic killings would have been possible without Hitchcock opening it up to a whole new emotional level in *Psycho.*"

He collaborated with Richard Franklin again on *Cloak and Dagger,* a kids' espionage film, and followed with the opportunity to write and—finally—direct *Fright Night.*

"There's an old saying that writers direct in self-defense," Holland laughs. "*Fright Night* marks the first time I can't say that the director didn't do it the way I intended it to be done. Oftentimes a film turns out very well, but it's not quite what I would have liked it to be. They may have been no worse, they may have been no better, but there were choices I would not have made. Whenever you have a mediating factor of someone else interpreting your material, it always changes and not always for the best."

One must wonder what the primary difference is between writing a film, and writing and directing one. In the first case, a person who "just" writes has to step away from it, but, in the second, he or she is seeing it through to completion.

"The quick answer is the hours," he responds, "but they are two different functions. As you know, writing is almost asocial, which is one of the wonderful things about it. Directing is an extremely social activity, because you're dealing with a large number of people. God, I'm one of the few people who could answer that honestly. . . . It's really a valid question. I think a lot of writers are mainly verbal; they hear dialogue. I think I tell the story in more of a visual way. In every one of my scripts, I've had at least three visual set pieces which move the story ahead visually with a minimal amount of dialogue. Often the director receives credit for that, even though it was written in the script. Because I think that way, perhaps I was a little bit more prepared to direct. Maybe more than a lot of other people.

"When you're writing, you can tell a story verbally, with words. When you're directing, you've got to let go of the words and figure out how to do it visually, where every image has to move the story forward. When you're writing a screenplay, you have to try to structure it where every scene moves it forward, but it's a very different conceptual way of thinking. It's very difficult to describe.

"On *Fright Night,* I finished writing the script, did the various revisions, took off my writer's hat, put on my director's hat, and sat down. I did my own storyboards, telling the story in a shot-by-shot breakdown, so that I could figure out how to do the film with a minimal number of set-ups that could be cut together in such a way as to give the effect that you want.

"Then there's working with the actors, which is something the writer never has to do. That goes to a question of not being married to your material and being willing to accommodate the cast and/or polish. It's like playwrights who have rehearsals and tryouts. This is because the way something reads on the page is not the way it sounds on its feet. The dramatic values can change, or the actor brings something new to it. You discover something you didn't think was there. It's really complicated, yet it's instinctive. Anyway, that's a very long answer to that question.

"The genesis of *Fright Night*," Holland explains, "was really my desire to do 'the boy who cried wolf,' but updated for the 1980s. I also have a tremendous affection for vampire strories, and those two interests seemed like a natural combination for a screenplay.

"One of the reasons that the genre faded was that vampire films were done as period pieces during their heyday, and nobody could figure out how to contemporize them. The parody is usually the last gasp of the genre, and I guess damn near ten years before *Fright Night* it was *Love at First Bite*, which I thought was very funny. Then I got outraged when I saw *The Hunger*. It was godawful, because it was a picture *ashamed* of the genre. It didn't mention the word "vampire" once. I wanted to bring it back.

"I tried to give the film some validity for a modern audience by rooting it in reality. For the first third, try selling the fact that this is happening in a real town, to a real family, to a real boy. Just to build up a willing suspension of disbelief for the audience. Once you've done that, you can get as fanciful as you want. I'm not sure what *Fright Night* is. It's a horror-fantasy-comedy, yet it doesn't poke fun at the genre, per se. It's very faithful to the traditions of the genre. I was determined to respect all the conventions of a traditional vampire story—coffin-beds, empty mirrors, and the like—but to place them in a contemporary context."

To create a sense of believability, Holland assembled a cast he felt could realistically translate his script to the screen. The results were even better than he had hoped.

"I was thrilled with every one of my actors," he says, "and there aren't a lot of directors who could say that. Every one of them played an important part in helping root the film in reality, and making it work so successfully."

He compares *Fright Night*'s mixture of horror and humor to John Landis's *An American Werewolf in London.*

"It's a good time," he says, "like a roller coaster with laughs and screams and more laughs. It's like 'Creatures Features'—something we all grew up with, and I think it's a very positive film, as strange as that sounds. I was also attracted to vampires in particular because they're a metaphor for seduction. Look at all the fun you have if you're a vampire. You get to sleep all day, sleep with any girl you want, and never die. That's not a bad life. There are a lot of psychological undertones that give it texture. I think if you took the vampire element out of *Fright Night,* you would have a very valid story about a teenaged kid who's losing his girl to a very cool older guy. If it was played on that level, it would be as psychologically valid as it is now.

"I sincerely wanted to differentiate between *Fright Night* and *Friday the 13th* and the other slasher films. With the horror, there's a lot of sweetness and humor. I wanted to give people a feeling of fun like I had when I was fourteen or fifteen and would sit home on Friday nights watching 'Creature Features,' making out with my girlfriend, and trying to feel her up at the same time. To get back to that sense of innocence. There were guys coming out of coffins on some of the most terrible sets you've ever seen . . ." he trails off with a laugh.

"I tried to mix in all those qualities as opposed to blood and gore. It is *not* blood and gore. That's not to say that the film doesn't deliver. There are some points there where you'll be jumping out of your seat, but I'm not doing it by throwing chicken blood all over the place. We worked together to make this a classy first-rate film."

Judging by the scripts he's written, we get the impression that Holland has a certain fascination with tortured individuals.

"Actually, I'm more interested in psychological suspense," he differs, "although Norman appeals to me. I love Norman, but who doesn't love Norman Bates? But, no, I wouldn't say so. What's interesting, what I like to do, is create a disturbing sympathy for the villain, and there should be something not very likeable about your hero. It's a more complex experience for the audience. A great example of that, I think, is Alfred Hitchcock's *Vertigo*. Kim Novack is the villain, but you start to feel sympathy for her. Jimmy Stewart is the victim and hero, but he's so obsessed that you start to dislike him. That is certainly the ambivalence you feel. It's what makes *Psycho II,* a lot of Hitchcock movies, and, hopefully, some of mine so successful creatively, and gives the characters some emotional resonance."

Although Holland went on to great success with *Child's Play,* he's avoided making sequels to both that film and *Fright Night.*

"What they usually do is make sequels cheaper, and they're derivative of the original," he says. "If someone says, 'Let's do a second one bigger and better,' then fine, but nobody ever does that. They all come and say, 'Let's make one that's smaller and make money off of the success of the first one,' and that's what happens. Does the audience love Chucky enough to see him killing more people? I don't think so, but the studio seems to think that they've got another Freddy Krueger here, and that's what's driving the idea of sequels. They think a property is pre-sold, so they don't even try.

"It's very hard," Holland adds. "Hollywood sort of looks upon horror movies as their money-making stepchildren. Yes, they're wonderful to make money with, but, God, they don't want their name on one of them. The studio system is not behind horror movies the way they are behind star movies or general audience popularity movies. The executives don't really have a taste for horror films, so it's difficult for them to judge them.

"Personally," he muses, "I think the reason I've probably enjoyed success with these films is that I bring a comedic and suspenseful sensibility to the horror genre. God knows that the genre scripts sent to me are either heavy effects or serial murders. There's not a lot that's original right now, and I need to feel that there's something special there to get me interested."

Roddy McDowall, a.k.a. Peter Vincent: *Fright Night*'s Vampire Hunter

He hunts vampires, but only in the movies. He introduces those fear flicks as the host of TV's *Fright Night Theatre.* And then, one dark and stormy evening, the horror cinema's famed "vampire killer" is swept into battle between local teenagers and the neighborhood bloodsucker. And *Fright Night* becomes something more than movies. It becomes terrifying reality for Peter Vincent.

"He's an absolutely marvelous character," declares the man who portrays him, Roddy McDowall, a veteran of nearly one hundred films. "I've never done anything like it, so it was extremely rewarding to me. The appeal to me is that Vincent is such a *terrible* actor. The poor dear is awful. He's just a very sweet man with no talent in a difficult situation, though he's able to rise to the occasion—like the Cowardly Lion."

While he feels that any explanation of his approach to the character would sound extremely "dumb" on the printed page, McDowall does mention that he drew Peter Vincent—named in tribute to Cushing and Price—partly from childhood memories.

"There were a couple of very bad actors," he says, "whom I absolutely adored as a child, and whose names today's audience wouldn't know. They were very bad actors from another time, and Peter Vincent is like them. He's full of sounds, but no content."

When writer/director Tom Holland approached him with the *Fright Night* script, McDowall's reaction was immediate enthusiasm. "I thought it was fascinating," he notes, "very imaginative and very good. Tom is a good director and writer, and all those elements were very conscientious. A great deal of hard work went into it."

The mixture of horror and humor in *Fright Night* may recall the similar structure of John Landis's *An American Werewolf in London,* but the comparison agitates McDowall.

"I never saw that film," he begins emphatically, "but I absolutely [despise] the idea of comparing one thing to something else. Nothing is worth anything unless it's taken on its own terms. It's one of the great pathetic sins that people go around in the world trying to compare this to that or something to something else. Why doesn't everybody just accept a thing on its own terms?

"All you can do is make a piece of product, sell it on its own terms, stand behind it, and hope that people will go see it. If you try to be like something else or appeal to any given group, then you can very easily end up being gratuitous and imitative. There's not much to be gained by that, and I think too much time is spent going around trying to be like someone else."

In addition, he doesn't appreciate *Fright Night* being labeled a "horror" film.

"Some people think *Snow White* is a horror movie, so I never quite know how to deal with that kind of labeling," McDowall says. "When I did the pilot for *Night Gallery,* I never looked at it as horror. It was a wonderful script and my character was just a lousy son of a bitch who turned people over to get what he wanted. I don't look at *Legend of Hell House* as horror either. It was just a story of people trying to exorcise a spirit from a haunted house.

"The so-called 'slice-and-dice' films are just gratuitous rubbish. I thought *The Omen* was a very good film. To me, horror is something Gothic, strange and peculiar, like a fairy tale. Approaching the premise of *Fright Night* realistically, it's *very* scary. The script made sense, dealing with a vampire living next door, just like a ghost—but I'm probably overstating my case because I think that too many things are labeled incorrectly."

Nevertheless, he feels that his character probably holds a great appeal for the audience. "I suppose every territory at various times has a horror host who introduces late night shows with rubbishy dialogue," he muses. "If the audience cringes watching them, they'll identify with the characters in *Fright Night.* Also, the kids in the cast [William Ragsdale, Amanda Bearse, and Stephen Geoffreys] are excellent. What sticks out in my mind is the group comraderie and closeness of everybody working on this film, really caring about *Fright Night* being good. And I think that comes across on the screen."

The actor reprised the role in the ultimately disappointing *Fright Night II,* though he did enjoy a second turn as the famed vampire killer. Could he see yet another return?

"He's a wonderful character and great fun," McDowall observes. "It's like after I did the first *Planet of the Apes* film. Nobody figured there would be five of them and a TV series. But there were, and they were all interesting to do, so you never can tell."

Chris Sarandon:
Fright Night's Vampire, Jerry Dandridge

In the past, cinematic vampires have been portrayed as pale-skinned ghouls wandering around cemeteries, draped in cumbersome black capes, and threatening to suck the blood out of any victims who happen by. Then, in the late 1970s, Frank Langella romanticized Bram Stoker's Dracula in the play and film of the same name, proving that vampires could be, above all else, charming.

Chris Sarandon contemporized this incarnation of evil to great effect in *Fright Night*, a film that has more in common with the Universal horror classics of the thirties and forties than the current crop of slice-and-dice productions that have proliferated in the genre.

In this updating of "The Boy Who Cried Wolf," Sarandon plays Jerry Dandridge, a vampire who will go to any means to make sure that his secret remains safe, including killing Charley Brewster, his teenaged next-door neighor, who has learned the truth.

"The thing that appeals to me about Jerry," explains Sarandon, who, since the time of this interview has starred in *The Princess Bride* and Tom Holland's *Child's Play,* "is that he's totally contemporary. That was something we all strived for, and something I found very interesting about the character, because he wasn't the Count of legend or Bram Stoker, but a guy who everybody knew and couldn't believe was being accused of being a vampire. He isn't the personification of pure evil that vampires are known to be."

What impressed the actor most about the character, was his multi-dimensional facets.

"Just think about this guy's problems," he says. "On the one hand, you've got somebody who's got something everybody would probably love to have, which is eternal life. Also, he's tremendously powerful physically, and attractive sexually. What he does, people are, for some reason, attracted to. But at the same time, how would you like to know that if people found out about you, nobody would really want to hang around you? That is, to spend eternity—but to spend eternity shunned by any normal kind of society; not being able to form any kind of normal human relationship. To be, in a way, damned to eternity. There's a sense of this guy's tragedy as well as his attractiveness."

This obvious enthusiasm is surprising, especially when one considers that the actor nearly turned the role down.

"I was sent the script by my agent and immediately sort of got sucked in by the plot, because it's wonderfully constructed and plotted," explains Sarandon. "After I read it, I said, 'Gee, this is going to make a great movie. It's a shame that I'm not really interested in playing this part.' The reasons for that are that over the last couple of years I've played a few villains and didn't want to get locked into playing another one. I thought the character was an interesting one, though I didn't think it was quite fleshed out. Despite my reservations, I had some conversations with Tom, we came up with some ideas, and I ended up doing it."

"I made a promise to Chris," adds Holland, "that I would make Jerry sensual and into a leading man, to show that side of him. He didn't want to do another wild and crazy character role."

Sarandon felt that what was missing was the character's haunted quality, part of which would come across in the playing, and that there were a few things needed in the script that would express this.

"The character's not so much the personification of pure evil, as he is a person who became a vampire by circumstances," he says. "We did all the groundwork for ourselves in terms of who this guy was and what happened; how it happened. Tom was very encouraging about that, to come up with that kind of life for the character so that he ultimately ends up more interesting for the audience."

Coming up with identifiable characters has been an objective of the actor's since graduating from the University of West Virginia, and, besides numerous stage roles, he's tried to achieve this goal via his various screen personas, from Al Pacino's gay lover in *Dog Day Afternoon* (which won him an Oscar nomination) and the rapist of *Lipstick,* to a tool of the devil in *The Sentinel,* a leading role with Goldie Hawn in *Protocol,* a comically evil prince in the aforementioned *Princess Bride,* and a homicide detective in *Child's Play.*

Bearing this in mind, one wonders if he had any aversion to the idea of playing a vampire, certainly one of the most bizarre roles he's been offered.

"It wasn't so much that," he counters, "but that the guy was such a bad guy. In a way he was, but in a way he wasn't. I think that I carried in some of my prejudices when I first read the script. Rather than read it in a very objective way, I read it in a much more 'what's it going to do for me?' way. Having played a couple of villains in the past, I was a little worried about it.

"I don't want to get locked into playing anything," he elaborates. "I don't want to be known as a heavy or as anything in particular, but just a good actor who can handle anything that comes along. Wishful thinking, but that's the image I would hope to have in the industry. That's something you cultivate over time by the choice of roles you take. Also, I think I underestimated the fact that in the movie I did just before *Fright Night, Protocol,* I was playing Mr. Total Straight Arrow. As nice a guy and as totally uncontroversial a character as you'll find anywhere. Considering that that's the one I did just before this, I think I needn't have worried so much. I came to realize that after a while."

The marathon makeup sessions came close to being a problem, but they enabled Sarandon to go from being the suave and good-looking Dandridge, to the snarling bat-like "spawn of Satan" during choice moments.

"We had certain stages of change," he reveals, "which had a lot to do with just how pissed off Jerry is at any particular moment . . . how provoked he is.

"I was stuck in makeup so goddamned much of the time," he sighs. "I had two weeks of eight-hour makeup calls, everyday. I'd go in at four in the morning and the makeup people would have to be in at three something. They'd start on me at four and I'd go to work at noon or one. Quite a remarkable experience. You either learn how to hypnotize yourself and meditate, or you become stark-raving mad.

"I tried to do the former," he laughs.

The big question was whether or not *Fright Night* could find a niche for itself in this age of slasher or splatter films.

"That's a good question," he says. "The feeling I had, and I have reasonably good instincts as an audience, is that it would work. When I first read the script, I couldn't put it down. I don't mean that as a cliché, I mean that for real. When I read that script, I remember sitting in the very chair I'm sitting in as we speak, my wife sitting in bed knitting, and I said, 'Sorry, honey. I know it's time to go in and start dinner, but I can't yet. I have to finish this.' I put it down like an hour and ten minutes later, and I figured that it was going to be a terrific movie."

Obviously, he was right.

The horror genre has intrigued Sarandon over the years, although he isn't really a fan of splatter films. Friends of his love those "really shocking" horror movies, but he is an aficionado of the older ones, such as the original *Dracula* and *Frankenstein*.

"And of practicioners like Hitchcock," he adds, "who really understood an audience. People who are much more interested in creating work which leaves a lasting impression. I'm much more interested in the resonance or haunting quality of the really good ones, and it'll be interesting to see if we've got one of those.

"There are a couple of things toward the end of the film where there's your requisite sort of special effects, bodies flying around and falling apart, and things like that. But that specifically comes about due to what's going on in the script. When I first read the script, there was, interestingly, very little real physical violence in it. What's so startling about it is you are in constant anticipation of a violent act, and that comes from good scriptwriting. The film also has a lot of humor, but it's intentional. It is a humor or irony in situations. Any humor comes out of the fact that the audience has invested a certain amount of emotional baggage with the characters, and if something funny happens they're going to laugh at that. We're having fun with it, but we're not making fun of it.

"Also, I think you'll find in this movie that in the first forty minutes or so there's only one violent act, and that's somebody sticking a pencil through somebody's hand. The rest of that time is spent leading up to something happening. You know something's got to happen, but nothing does. To me, that's much more effective, a kind of Hitchcockian approach to that sort of material. What's much more important is how you lead up to the act rather than the act itself. It's not what you see, but what you've dreaded seeing," he explains.

Could he see himself returning as Jerry Dandridge?

"I might, but who knows?" Sarandon closes prophetically. "It's an interesting character for me. I could perceive bringing him back, but it would depend on the circumstances."

INDEX

Dark Shadows soap opera
(*continued*)
popularity of, 153, 155, 161
Dave's World, 32
Dawson's Creek, 18
Dead Man on Campus, 35
Dog Day Afternoon, 196
Dr. Phibes Rises Again, 180
Dracula movies, 62
Bela Lugosi in, 169–171
Christopher Lee in, 171–174
director Badham's *Dracula,* 183
Drusilla
as Angel's victim, 110, 115, 131
introduction of, 102–103
Juliet Landau as, 45–46
Kendra's battle with, 132–133
as Ms. Calendar, 134
premonitions of, 126–127
Spike and, 109, 112, 113, 134
Ducote, Andrew, 127
Duncan, Lois, 20

E
Edmonds, Louis, 149
Elvira, 180
Emmy award, Gellar's daytime, 9, *10*–11
Episode guide in this book
season one, 73–97
season two, 98–135
Ethan, 108, 112
The Evil Dead, 60

F
Facts of Life, 13
Family Ties, 13
Fatal Beauty, 184
Fight sequences, 120
Buffy's battles with Angel, 122, 132, 134–135
Gellar's zealousness in, 13, 24
in "When She Was Bad," 99
Film version of *Buffy,* vii
Kristy Swanson in, 25, 75
writer Whedon on, 52–53, 63
Fincher, David, 56
Ford (Buffy's former boyfriend), 109–111
Fox, Michael J., 24, 26
Frankenstein, 170, 197
French, Ms., 80, 81
Frid, Jonathan
on *Dark Shadows* audition, 150–151
profile of, 155–164
on vampire role, 152–153
Friday the 13th, 189
Fright Night, 183–184
Chris Sarandon in, 183, 194–198
Roddy McDowall in, 184, 191–193
writer Tom Holland on, 184–191

G
Gellar, Sarah Michelle, 3–27
on Buffy character, 13–14, 15–16
as Burger King girl, 4–6
as daytime Emmy award winner, 9, *10*–11
discovery of, 3–4
on *I Know What You Did Last Summer,* 17, 18–22
high school and junior high years, 13–14
on horror films, 17–18
in *Scream 2,* 22–24
on series creator Joss Whedon, 24, 26
as soap opera star, 8–11
as Tae Kwon Do brown belt, 6, 11, 13
on teenagers' interest in Buffy, 14–16
television appearances of, 6–7
Web sites, 141–142
on year two of the series, 26–27
on young actors, 4, 6
Gershman, Michael, 125
Giles
as Angel's prisoner, 132, 133
Anthony Stewart Head as, 42–44
as Buffy's Watcher, 42–43, 65, 75, 111
in "The Dark Age" episode, 111–112
darker nature of, 108
discovery of Ms. Calendar's dead body by, 127
Ms. Calendar as love interest for, 42, 101, 112, 126

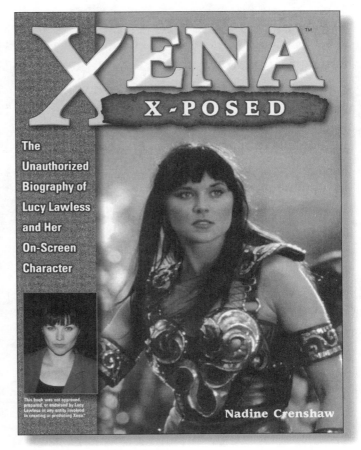

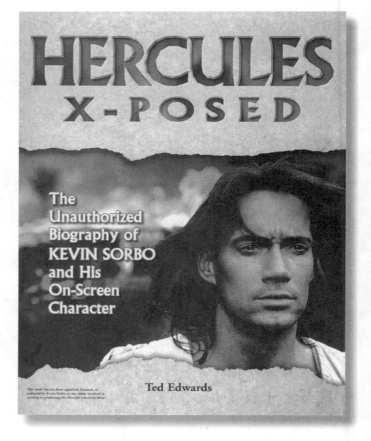

Unrestricted Access to Section One's Sexiest Operative

She's smart; she's sexy; she's dangerous. She's television's most lethal heroine. You want to know more about her—and about her real-life persona, Peta Wilson—but until now everything about her has been classified. Now, access has been granted. With *La Femme Nikita X-Posed* you will discover such confidential information as:

- **How the TV series measures up to its two big-screen predecessors**
- **What psychological background actress Peta Wilson created for her character**
- **How cult sensation Roy Dupuis got cast as Nikita's fellow operative, Michael**
- **And more!**

Covering every explosive episode to date, this book cuts through the mystery and will give you a glimpse into the soul of television's most captivating femme fatale.

TED EDWARDS

LA FEMME NIKITA
X-POSED

THE **UNAUTHORIZED** BIOGRAPHY OF
PETA WILSON AND HER ON-SCREEN
CHARACTER

This book has not been approved, licensed, or endorsed by PETA WILSON or any entity involved in creating or producing LA FEMME NIKITA™ the television show.

ISBN 0-7615-1454-6 / paperback / 208 pages
U.S. $16.00 / Can. $21.95

PRIMA

**To order, call (800) 632-8676 or
visit us online at www.primapublishing.com**

To Order Books

Please send me the following items:

Quantity	Title	Unit Price	Total
_____	_____	$ _____	$ _____
_____	**Xena X-Posed**	$ 16.95	$ _____
_____	**Hercules X-Posed**	$ 16.00	$ _____
_____	**La Femme Nikita X-Posed**	$ 16.00	$ _____
_____	_____	$ _____	$ _____

Subtotal	$ _____
Deduct 10% when ordering 3–5 books	$ _____
7.25% Sales Tax (CA only)	$ _____
8.25% Sales Tax (TN only)	$ _____
5% Sales Tax (MD and IN only)	$ _____
7% G.S.T. Tax (Canada only)	$ _____
Shipping and Handling*	$ _____
Total Order	$ _____

*Shipping and Handling depend on Subtotal.

Subtotal	Shipping/Handling
$0.00–$14.99	$3.00
$15.00–$29.99	$4.00
$30.00–$49.99	$6.00
$50.00–$99.99	$10.00
$100.00–$199.99	$13.50
$200.00+	Call for Quote

Foreign and all Priority Request orders:
Call Order Entry department
for price quote at 916-632-4400

This chart represents the total retail price of books only
(before applicable discounts are taken).

By Telephone: With MC, Visa, or American Express, call 800-632-8676 or 916-632-4400.
Mon–Fri, 8:30–4:30.

WWW: http://www.primapublishing.com

By Internet E-mail: sales@primapub.com

By Mail: Just fill out the information below and send with your remittance to:

**Prima Publishing
P.O. Box 1260BK
Rocklin, CA 95677**

Name _____

Address _____

City _____ State _____ ZIP _____

MC/Visa#/American Express _____ Exp. _____

Check/money order enclosed for $ _____ Payable to Prima Publishing

Daytime telephone _____

Signature _____